Dare to Be Scared

Dare to Be Scared

Thirteen Stories to Chill and Thrill

Robert D. San Souci

Illustrations by David Ouimet

SCHOLASTIC INC.
New York Toronto London Auckland Sydney
Mexico City New Delhi Hong Kong Buenos Aires

ISBN 0-439-74625-6

Published by Scholastic Inc., 557 Broadway, New York, NY 10012,
by arrangement with Carus Publishing.

12 11 10 9 8 7 6 5 4 7 8 9 10/0

Printed in the U.S.A. 40

First Scholastic printing, March 2005

Designed by Anthony Jacobson

For all the readers I have met who
love to be scared:

This book is for you!

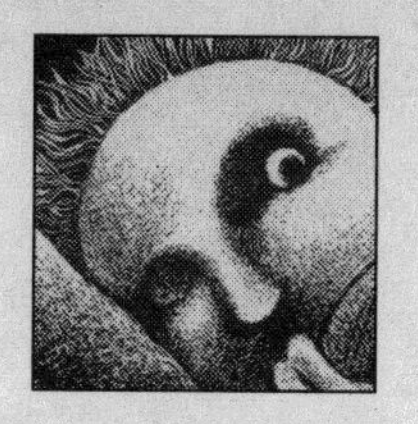

Contents

Nighttown

Sammy was dreaming; he was sure of it.

He was walking around the city that he had explored with his parents earlier. In a way the streets were the same, the buildings were the same—painted bright orange and blue and yellow and pink. And there were lots of palm trees to remind him that he was on vacation with his family on a beautiful island in the Caribbean Sea.

But everything was all wrong, too. It was night, but the sky had no moon or stars, so he couldn't tell where the light—brighter than real moonlight—came from. All the streetlights were dark. And the streets were empty. Before, they had been crowded with people and funny little cars and donkeys. Now, no matter which way he turned, he saw no one. Doors were closed; windows were dark or had their shutters fastened. It was creepy.

But, so far at least, Sammy was happy that it was still only a dream, not a *nightmare.*

He kept walking, since there was no reason to stop. He kept hoping that he would find the main street and see the Beach View Hotel where he was staying with his parents. He had the idea that if he could find his way back to where he was really asleep in his bed, he would wake up and forget this strange dream.

Of course, the strangest part was *knowing* he was in a dream, and thinking he could get out of it, if only he could find his way back.

He turned a corner. Halfway down the street he saw a man leaning against a wall. He was dressed in a white suit and white hat and white shoes. Sammy knew he wasn't supposed to talk to strangers. But he was in his own dream now, so he decided everyday rules didn't apply.

"Excuse me, sir," the boy said politely. "Could you tell me the way to the Beach View Hotel?"

"Sure thing," said the man. Then he grinned and showed his teeth. They were three times as long as teeth should be. And they were sharp.

Sammy didn't wait. He ran and ran, up one street and down another. He was afraid the fellow with the horrible teeth was chasing him. He kept looking over his shoulder, which was why he ran into the black police officer, dressed in the white coat and shorts and high helmet all police officers wore here.

"Stop boy!" the man said, grabbing his arm. "Why are you running?"

"Sorry!" said Sammy. "I was frightened by a man whose teeth were as long as this!" And the boy moved his fingers far enough apart to show the policeman.

The policeman nodded. "But were they as long as this?" He grinned, and Sammy saw the policeman's teeth were twice as long as the first man's and even sharper.

With a yell the boy twisted away from the policeman's grasp and began running again. He heard the policeman laughing behind him. A turn to the right, then a turn to the left, and he was in another strange street. He didn't stop running until he could no longer hear the awful laughter.

There was a church in this street. A priest was sweeping the steps. He had on a white robe, but he also had on tennis shoes and a New York Giants baseball cap. He seemed friendly and funny as he waved to Sammy. But Sammy didn't go too close until he saw the priest's teeth. They looked just the right size.

"Poor boy!" said the man. "You look like you've run a ten-mile race. Is anything wrong?"

Still panting, Sammy said, "I met two men. One had teeth this long"—and he showed the priest how long.

"Oh, my!" the priest cried.

"Then," Sammy went on, "I met a policeman who had teeth this long!" Again he showed the priest how long.

"My, my, my!" exclaimed the priest with a little grin. "Those are very long. But not as long as *these!*" Suddenly his grin was big as a pumpkin's, and his teeth were growing longer by the minute.

Away ran Sammy, promising himself not to stop and talk to anyone. He would just keep running until he woke up.

The next street he ran into was the main street. And not far away was the Beach View Hotel. In the middle of the dark buildings, all of the hotel lights were blazing, as if to guide him home. Feeling safer every minute, Sammy ran across the empty hotel lobby, took the elevator to the seventh floor, and saw the door to suite 710—the room where his family was staying—just down the hall.

It was unlocked. He tiptoed inside. The living room looked just as he remembered it. The door to his parents' room was closed, but he could hear his mother's soft breathing and his father's light snoring just inside. He quickly opened the door to his own bedroom. There he saw his real self asleep in the soft light that came through the window where a curtain was only half closed.

"Wake up! Wake up!" he shouted to his sleeping self. But the sleeper only turned over and seemed likely to go on sleeping. "Get me out of this dream," Sammy pleaded with the dreamer.

When he saw that his words weren't having any effect, Sammy reached over to try and shake himself awake. As soon as his dream-hand touched his real shoulder, his whole body jerked as if he had gotten a tremendous electric shock.

"Whoa!" he cried, sitting up in bed. He was breathing heavily, and he could feel his heart pounding. He swiped the back of his hand across his sweaty forehead. "I'm

HOTEL

back!" he assured himself. A minute later, his parents appeared at the door.

"What are you shouting about?" asked his father, hurrying to one side of the bed.

"Are you all right?" asked his mother, sitting on the other side of his bed.

Sammy rubbed his eyes. "I had a weird dream," he said. "I guess it was a *nightmare*. Anyhow, I was being chased by all these guys with sharp teeth that got longer and longer and longer."

"Sounds like a nightmare to me," his father chuckled. "How long were those teeth? As long as *these?*"

"Or *these?*" asked his mother.

And just before Sammy pulled the covers over his head and began to scream, he saw through the window that the night sky had light but no moon or stars.

The Dark, Dark House

The four boys—Eddie, Joe, JB, and Randy—looked at their friend Peter. "Remember," Joe said, "The deal is that you've got to go all the way into the big bedroom upstairs and write the date in chalk beside the closet there."

"And put your initials," added JB.

"That will prove you were there," Joe finished.

All five turned to look down the hill toward the old Brewster house. The deserted place—all the kids in town were sure it was haunted—had been empty since long before Peter and the others had been born. Soon it would be torn down to make way for new town houses. Bulldozers and trucks had already begun clearing and leveling the vacant lots that surrounded the solitary house. Though the moonlit Brewster house stood stubbornly amid the surrounding changes, soon the wreckers would come and tear it down. The neighborhood kids were looking forward to *that*. But tonight, the boys had come to check out one last time the story that a ghost—or *something*—prowled the house at midnight.

All the boys had been brave enough to explore the house during the day, even though signs warned trespassers away. But they had gone as a group. None of them wanted to be alone inside—even when the sun was shining. Only a lot of double-daring, and the promise of collecting the allowances of the other four boys, had made Peter agree to make this midnight visit alone.

The boys had been planning the adventure for days, deciding how they could sneak out and meet without any parents finding out. So far, everything had worked just fine. Yet—though he didn't tell his friends—Peter was beginning to wish that something had gone wrong and that he had been grounded for the night.

But here they all were, there was the house, and Joe was saying, "It's almost time. Unless you're going to chicken out on us."

"No way," said Peter. He was annoyed that his dry-as-a-bone throat made his voice sound like a frog's croak. Joe smirked. Peter ignored him and made a show of patting his jeans pockets to be sure he had his flashlight and the chalk, so he could write the date and his initials in the big upstairs bedroom. That was where, supposedly, someone had been killed by a monster or scared to death by a ghost or simply vanished. There were as many different stories about the room as there were kids to share them.

Even as he made a show of being brave, Peter remembered the worst stories he had heard. But there was no getting out of the challenge now. No midnight monster could be as bad as having his friends call him chicken.

So he started walking down the hillside toward the old road and the crumbling house on the other side. He looked back only once, and saw his friends sitting side by side, sharing the candy bars Eddie had brought and watching him to see when his courage would give out. They were all sure he'd never make it through the loose board on the window that kids used to sneak in and out during the day.

"I'll show you all," Peter whispered.

Though he walked as slowly as he could and still not look like he was scared, he reached the road, and then the rusted iron gate, and finally the front porch far too soon.

He had been in the house with the others during the day. Now he tried to tell himself that it really wouldn't be that different by night. And the stories about monsters and ghosts and junk were only *stories*.

Just before he lifted the board that would let him slip inside, he turned and gave a big, defiant wave to his friends on the hill. He saw them wave back. They seemed so tiny in the moonlight. The dark, dark house seemed higher and wider than it ever looked in the sunshine.

He climbed through the window. Behind him, the board dropped back into place with a soft *chunk* that made him jump.

The room inside was dark, dark, *dark*. He snapped on his flashlight, but the beam was weak. Now he remembered that he had meant to get new batteries before he came here. The light was only a thin spear of brightness stabbing into the black. It picked out the side of a wooden box, some fallen plaster, and the corner of a rug so old and mildewed that it looked like it was growing on the floor.

Something in the hall beyond the room went *chink-chink*. Peter froze.

"Hello," he said, his voice little more than a whisper. "Is anybody there?" His words seemed to stick in his throat, which had gone too tight to let out much of the sound.

Nobody answered.

Taking a deep breath, he crossed the dark, dark room and entered the even darker hall.

"Hello," he said, louder this time.

Nobody answered.

Down the gloomy hall he went.

Up the dark, dark stairs—jumping with every step that creaked—and most of them did.

At the top he paused to listen. Silence, except for the faint *chink-chink* sound. He angled the flashlight beam up and saw an old light fixture in the stairwell ceiling. Its hanging glass beads, wrapped in spider webs, made the chinking sound as they jostled together in a stray draft. He could feel the same cold air on the back of his neck, and he shivered, as if a ghost had puffed its icy breath on him. He fought the urge to run away. He was too close to his goal to back out now.

The door to the bedroom he had to enter was closed. He reached for the knob, half afraid that he would see it begin to turn by itself, as something inside got ready to pop out. That's the sort of thing that happened in the scary DVDs he loved to watch with Randy and Randy's older brothers.

"Don't stop now," he urged himself.

He pushed the door wide on the darkest space yet. Across the room, the door to a dark, dark closet was wide open. A little moonlight came through windows caked with dust. That was good, because the batteries in his flashlight gave out at that moment. But the wall between the shadowy closet and the dark corner caught just enough light so he could see to write. Quickly he got out his chalk and scribbled the date and his initials.

Something sighed in the dark, dark closet.

Peter turned. He couldn't get his feet moving.

There! He was sure he had again heard something breathing or whispering in the inky interior.

Something soft fell in the closet. Peter yelled.

Out jumped a dark, dark—

Nothing.

"Smooth move, chicken," he mocked himself. He tried to shake the flashlight back into life. No luck.

He turned to go. Something soft *tunked* in the closet.

"Fool me once, shame on you," he said, repeating one of his mother's favorite sayings. "Fool me twice, shame on me." He turned to go.

Something dark and big put a cold, hairy hand on his shoulder.

"Nobody's fooling anyone," said a voice as cold as the hand.

Peter yelled, twisted free of the hand, and ran out of the bedroom. He paused just long enough to slam the door shut. It stuck for a moment. He heard the *something* rattling the knob. He half stumbled, half fell down the stairs. He was raising the window board when he heard something come bumping, thumping, galumphing down the steps behind him. He threw himself out through the opening, bruising his shoulder. For a minute his jeans cuff caught on a nail, but he ripped it free.

Now he was running down the path, past the rusty iron gate, across the road. Without stopping, he looked back. Two hairy arms slammed the board off the window, sending it flying into a bush. A huge form squeezed through a moment later. The giant, shadowy shape chased him.

Peter ran faster, struggling up the hill toward his friends. But if he thought they were going to help him, he was wrong. The minute they saw that something was following him, Eddie, Joe, JB, and Randy scattered in four different directions, each of them yelling his lungs out.

The shadowy thing was catching up.

Fear gave Peter an extra burst of speed. He crossed the top of the hill and charged down the brush-covered slope on the far side. He took the paths between the bushes and briars that were boy-sized, but not wide enough for the big shadowy *something* that was chasing him. He heard brambles and branches snap and crackle as they snagged and caught at the monster, slowing it down.

Across the edge of the cemetery, through the park, and onto the sidewalks of town Peter ran, thinking only of getting home.

When he was just a few doors from his house, and his legs were so tired he could hardly move them, he dared to turn and look back down Maple Street.

The sidewalks and road were empty. Under the full moon, nothing moved except a cat darting from one side of the street to the other. He had lost the thing. He was safe. Just a few more steps to home.

Peter turned into his own yard.

He had just put his foot on the front step when the big, dark something grabbed him with two big, hairy hands!

"What's the matter?" it rasped. "Don't you *like* me?"

The Caller

It was hot at Aunt Margaret's funeral. Being in church had been tiring, but this was worse. Lindsay Walters had to stand in the hot sun, sweating in the ugly, black, too-heavy dress her parents had made her wear, while the minister prayed on and on. The bunches of flowers draped across the coffin had wilted. Lindsay almost giggled as she thought of Aunt Margaret in her coffin turning golden brown like a big biscuit in a toaster oven.

Lindsay was angry because she *should* be at Missy's, helping her best friend get ready for a party. Except for her mother and father and two brothers, there were only a few dried-up men and ladies from the old folks' home. And *they* got to sit on folding chairs, Lindsay thought, while we have to *stand*.

A cell phone rang. Lindsay knew from the stupid "Yankee Doodle Went to Town" tune that it was her father's. He went red in the face. At least *she* knew enough to turn hers off so it wouldn't ring in church or at the cemetery. Her father pulled his phone out of its carrying case, shut off the signal, but glanced at the caller's phone number. He made a face and glanced at his watch. Then he put the phone back in its case and looked across at the minister. Happily, Lindsay saw that the reverend was just about done.

As soon as the final prayers were said, and the minister was patting her mother's hand, Lindsay ducked behind a tree, took out her own cell phone, and dialed Missy's number. It was busy. Probably her friend was making plans with Noelle or Candice for the party. She made a face at the phone, turned, and bumped into her father, who was talking into his phone. He shooed her back to her mother, while he kept talking. *Like my calls aren't that important,* Lindsay thought sourly.

Her mother introduced her to some boring old ladies. She had to nod and look sad as they yakked about her aunt, while her mother and brothers talked to the minister. When her father returned, Lindsay asked, "Can we go now?"

"I just have to make one more call," her father said. He moved off to where they couldn't overhear him.

When the last old lady and the minister had gone, Lindsay begged her mother to "Please, please, *please* make Daddy get off the phone so we can go!"

"Stop whining," her mother said. But she waved impatiently at Lindsay's father. "Show some respect," she ordered Lindsay's brothers, who were trying to trip each other in one of their weird games. Darren fell on his seat a few feet from Aunt Margaret's coffin. She would be buried when they had left. David laughed. Their mother ordered all of them to the car, then marched over to where Mr. Walters was still talking on the phone. The kids could see she wanted to get going. She made their father end his call. Now both of them were angry. Mr. Walters shoved his phone into his coat pocket, not into its holster. "All right, let's get this show on the road," he said. But he had to go after Darren and David, who had climbed out of the car and were now playing tag.

Some people from the funeral had stopped by the house. Lindsay and her brothers had to sit around and smile while their sad-faced parents and guests drank coffee and tea and talked about how nice Aunt Margaret had been.

"As long as you didn't make her angry," said Mr. Walters with a sharp laugh. "I remember as a kid that she could be a holy terror if she thought someone had been rude or was lying or cruel." Lindsay knew what he was talking about. Her aunt had a real temper. Lindsay thought of the woman in heaven, terrorizing the angels for not being holy enough. She'd tune up the heavenly choir, all right, or feathers would fly. It was all the girl could do to keep from laughing aloud at the picture in her mind.

But the guests finally left. Lindsay ran to her room to change so that her father could drive her to Missy's party.

When she was ready, she opened her red-velvet jewel case and took out Aunt Margaret's ring, set with real diamonds in white gold. She had always loved it, and Aunt Margaret had promised it to her just before she died. Her mother had wanted to keep it until Lindsay was older, but Lindsay had thrown one of her best tantrums and said that the old woman had wanted her to wear it always. (She had made up that part, but it seemed to work on her mother, who told her only to wear the ring at special times. Well, showing off to Missy and Noelle and Candice and the others was special!)

Her cell phone, beside the jewel box, rang.

There was some strange crackling, then a lot of whispering, sounding like a crowd. Finally a voice so tired and dry and old that it was hard to tell if it was a man or a woman said, "Lindsay, darling, this is Aunt Margaret."

"Right! Nice try, Missy, guys—see you in a few minutes." Lindsay hung up and put her phone in her party bag. Slipping the ring in her jeans pocket, so her parents wouldn't see, she rushed down the steps two at a time.

"Where's Dad? He's supposed to drive me to Missy's."

"He's out in the car looking for his cell phone," her mother said. "It fell out of his pocket."

Sighing at the hopelessness of all grownups, Lindsay helped her father search the car; but the phone was gone. He was in a bad mood. She was glad she was spending the night at Missy's after the party.

Aunt Margaret's ring helped make up for arriving late. All the girls at Missy's were jealous of the real diamonds on Lindsay's finger. She forgot about their phone joke.

"I hated to go to that smelly old folks' home," Lindsay told them. "I just pretended I wanted to go, because I wanted this ring. But Aunt Margaret thought I was nice, so she left me her ring when she died last week."

Her cell phone rang. She grabbed her purse from beside the couch and answered it.

Lots of static, more whispers, then the same dried-up voice saying, "Lindsay, this is Aunt Margaret. I must talk to you."

Clearly it wasn't her friends trying to trick her. That meant it had to be Darren and David. She covered the mouthpiece and whispered, "It's my creepy brothers pretending to be my aunt's ghost." The others rolled their eyes, knowing what jerks younger brothers could be.

"Is it *really* you, Aunt Margaret?" asked Lindsay, trying to sound little-girl scared, playing along with the game.

"Yes. I just wanted to hear your sweet voice again."

How corny could they get? Lindsay wondered.

"You were always my favorite. You loved me best."

Lindsay held up the ring and wiggled her fingers as she talked. "Well, it was really your ring I loved." The other girls put their hands over their mouths and giggled. "I hated going to that place where you stayed. And I hated it when you kissed me, because your breath always smelled like sour milk or tuna fish. And all that stuff you told me about when you were young was as boring as my jerks of brothers talking about football scores. So thanks for the ring and goodbye, *Aunt Margaret!"* Lindsay disconnected the phone.

She punched **69* to see where her brothers were calling from. The read-out was her father's cell phone number.

"They're using my dad's phone that he was looking for. They're never supposed to touch it. They must have found it in the car. I'm going to see that they get *so busted* for this when I get home."

When the party ended and the other girls left after dinner, Missy's parents said they were going to visit neighbors. They left the number where they could be reached, even though Missy reminded them that she and Lindsay often stayed home alone. As soon as they were gone, the girls went upstairs to Missy's room to call their friends and talk about boys and clothes and MTV. Lying at opposite ends of Missy's bed, they chatted into their cell phones.

Lindsay was just about to dial her boyfriend of the week, when her phone rang.

"Lindsay, I am very disappointed in you." The same voice.

"Get lost!"

"I don't think you deserve my ring. I'm coming to get it back."

"Get real!" She broke the connection. The read-out showed her father's cell phone. She punched the number, but the line just rang and rang. She hung up and dialed her home. Her mother answered.

"Mom," she said, "Darren and David found Dad's phone. They've been using it to call and bug me. They just did it again."

"That's not possible," said her mother. "They've been watching a game for the past hour. And your father is sure he dropped his phone at the cemetery this afternoon. He's going to check there tomorrow morning." Now her mother sounded worried, "Do you think it's a real crank caller?"

"The read-out shows Dad's cell phone number," Lindsay explained. "But—"

There was a burst of static. The phone went dead. Missy looked up as her phone went dead too. The lights in the house flickered, dimmed, then went out. "Blackout," said Missy. All the other houses in the neighborhood were dark.

"I don't think that would shut off our phones," said Lindsay.

"Well, it did," said Missy. "Anyhow, I was bored with what Noelle was telling me. And this is cool. We can tell ghost stories."

"I don't want to," said Lindsay, wishing she were home and not spending the night in a lightless house. The cut-off conversation with her mother had worried her more than she liked to admit. But Missy's folks would be home soon, she decided.

"Chicken!" her friend teased.

There was a knocking downstairs at the front door. It had an odd, echoing sound to it. *Thunk. Thunk. Thunk.*

Missy got up to answer it.

"Don't!" cried Lindsay. She couldn't say why she was frightened, but in truth she was suddenly feeling scared.

"You are *so* stupid," said Missy. "My folks forgot their keys or something. Probably the doorbell doesn't work like the phones don't."

"Please, don't go!"

"Stay here, if you're so scared," said Missy, shaking her head. "What a wuss!" She left. A moment later Lindsay heard her running down the stairs two at a time.

Lindsay closed the bedroom door and locked it. She heard the front door open and slam a moment later. She thought she heard a soft sound, like something heavy being dropped. Then quiet. She listened harder, hoping to hear the sound of familiar voices. But there was only silence.

Her cell phone rang.

She snatched it up, hoping it was her mother calling back.

"Lindsay, I've come for my ring, you unhappy child. I'm at the foot of the stairs right now. Let's play that game I played when you were a little girl. The one your father told me not to play, because it frightened you so? But you loved it—you loved being scared. Don't you like being scared anymore?"

"Missy? Are you playing a trick on me? This isn't funny."

But Missy's phone was still on the bed where she had left it.

"One step, two—I'm coming for you," said the voice in the phone.

Thump, thump on the stairs.

"Three steps, four—better lock the door."

Two more *thumps*.

But Lindsay had already locked the door. Part of her wanted to shut off the phone, but she didn't dare.

"Five steps, six—say your prayers quick."

If the phone were working, Lindsay thought, she could call for help. She hung up and dialed her home phone number. It was answered on the third ring.

"Seven steps, eight—not long to wait," said her mother's voice.

She hung up and dialed 911.

"Nine steps, ten—we're near the end," said a man's voice.

She hung up and threw the phone onto the bed beside Missy's.

"Eleven, twelve, and one step more—too late for you, I'm at the door!" It was Aunt Margaret's angry voice, the one she'd used when Darren and David's football broke a window in her house before she moved to the old folks' home.

Someone rattled the door handle, found it locked, and knocked loudly.

THUMP! THUMP! THUMP!

"Go away! Leave me alone! I didn't mean what I said!" Lindsay started to cry.

"Gotcha!" cried Missy through the door. "You're crying! This is better than telling ghost stories! Wait till Noelle and Candice hear I made you cry. You and that stupid ring you think is so cool."

Angry at how she'd been tricked, Lindsay wiped away her tears and yanked open the door. "I never want to talk to you again!" she yelled.

But it wasn't Missy holding Lindsay's father's phone in a muddy hand as the lights came on.

The Double-Dare

By the third week of June, the boys were staying out in the park until almost dark playing tag or softball or just messing around. They would wait until they knew they couldn't stretch the fun any longer without getting in trouble. Then they'd play the "Dare" game.

The five of them—Pat Marshall, Danny Geertz, Tay Green, Larry Chan, and Greg Strickland—would gather at the far side of the park where a patch of trees and brush had been allowed to run wild. It was almost as if the park workers stayed away from it, except to pick up the papers and other debris that caught on the bushes and in the tall grass along the edges. It looked like there was no way in or out of the tangled trees and shrubs, but the boys knew there was a zigzag path that ran the length of it. And exactly in the middle was a circle where nothing grew except some blotchy crab grass. Anyone following the path knew he was halfway to the end when he reached what Larry had nicknamed the "dead zone."

The friends would stand at one end of the path and tell all the stories they'd heard about the ghost of an Indian or a woman without a head who haunted the dead zone. They'd talk about weird noises or strange shadows or green or blue lights people had seen along the path. They recalled the catalog of horrors each time—adding newer and gorier details with each telling—then began daring each other to run the length of the path after sunset.

Sometimes they did too good a job scaring each other. No one would take the dare. At other times, they'd gang up on one or the other, calling "Chicken!" and making clucking noises, until the one being teased couldn't stand it any longer. Into the tree shadows he'd go, while the others ran along the edge of the grove to meet him at the other end.

In the weeks since school had let out, Pat, Danny, Tay, and Larry had all run through at least twice. Pat, the leader of the group, had run through four times. The only one who hadn't gone through was Greg Strickland. The boys called him "Stickman" because he was so tall and skinny. He looked like a stick figure with big round circles—his thick glasses—for eyes. Though he was only going into third grade, and the others would be in fourth, he was as tall as they were.

Normally, the soon-to-be-fourth graders would have kept a "baby" out of their group. But Greg always had the latest games to play on the fanciest computer the boys had seen. He lived with his divorced dad, who worked for a big electronics firm, designing computer games. And Greg's father never hassled them about "getting out in the fresh air," like the others' parents did, when they were happy to play computer games indoors for hours on end.

Because they didn't want to lose access to Greg's games, the boys let him tag along with them. And they didn't double-dare him to run through the trees. But they *did* enjoy telling him stories of things they were sure they had seen as they zigzagged through the branches and brambles. They'd nudge each other as Greg grew popeyed when Pat told about the man's face made of leaves and weeds that he saw a minute before an arm like a tree branch clawed at him. Proudly he showed the four scratches—now four dark scabs—that proved his story. "He almost got me, but I broke free," said Pat.

"No way!" said Greg.

"Way!" said Pat, pushing his scratched arm right up to Greg's face.

But the game of dare was called that night because of Diana, Pat's sixteen-year-old sister. Their parents had sent her to drag him home. For good measure, she warned the others that they'd be in trouble themselves if they didn't get home. "Your folks have already started calling around for you," she said to the others. Then she asked her brother, "Are you playing your stupid game? I swear one day one of you is going to poke out an eye or break his neck running around there in the dark."

"You sound like Mom," Pat replied. "Only worse."

His friends, who were tagging along to the park gates, chuckled.

"Anyhow, you shouldn't mess around in places like this. Not tonight. It's Midsummer's Eve. Tomorrow is June twenty-first. Midsummer."

"So?" her brother asked.

"It's the longest day of the year. A lot of people believe it's a magic time. It has to do with nature power and spirits of the woods and an old god or something they called the Green Man, who made things grow."

Pat rolled his eyes. "You are *weird!*" To his friends he said, "She's got all these crystals and she burns incense in her room even though Mom told her not to, and she reads all these weird books and magazines and finds stuff on the Internet—except Dad looked at some of the sites she was visiting and made her stop. Didn't he, Weird Woman?"

"Grow up," she said. "Actually, it might be a good thing if something got you. I wouldn't have to *baby*-sit anymore. But I couldn't imagine any nature spirit *stupid* enough to take you away, even if I *paid* it to."

They had reached the edge of the park. After waving and shouting "See you tomorrow," the boys went their separate ways.

But Diana's talk had got Pat thinking. The next evening, Pat sent Greg—the group's errand boy—to buy some potato chips and candy and sodas with money they'd all chipped in. When the youngest boy was gone, Pat told Danny, Tay, and Larry, "Tonight we're going to double-dare the Stickman to make the run."

"But he won't," Larry said. "He's too scared."

"If we tell him we won't be friends anymore," said Pat, "he'll have to."

"But if he won't, and we aren't friends, then we won't get to play with his computer," said Tay.

"I'm bored with that stuff," said Pat. "His dad hasn't brought home any new games for weeks. And just think how scary it's going to be for him."

"Yeah," said Danny, who always backed up Pat. "He'll probably wet his pants he'll be so scared."

By the time the Stickman brought back their snacks, Larry and Tay were convinced.

The younger boy guessed something was up from the way the others looked at him and grinned.

"It's Midsummer," Pat said, trying to sound serious. The boys standing behind him struggled not to laugh. "You heard what my sister said. Tonight everything in there comes alive," and he pointed to the rapidly darkening trees. "Whoever makes the run this time has to be the bravest runner, because it's going to be scariest tonight. Stickman, I dare, dare, *double-dare* you."

"Double-dare, double-dare, double-dare," the other boys echoed.

Greg took a step back from them, shaking his head, "I can't!" he said. He sounded like he was going to cry. This encouraged the others.

"If you don't take the dare," said Pat, "you can't be our friend anymore."

"We've all made the run," added Danny, "except you."

"I don't know the way. I've never been in there," said Greg in a voice that had shriveled to a whisper now.

"Just follow the path. When you get to the dead zone at the middle, you'll know you're halfway home," Pat said. "Make up your mind, or we're outta here." The four older boys drew together, making it clear there was no room among them for a coward.

"All right," said Greg, sounding ready to cry. Pat elbowed Danny, enjoying the other boy's fear.

They led Greg, two on either side, like guards leading a condemned prisoner, to the head of the tree-shadowed path.

They were amused at how his skinny legs and arms trembled. They could see that he was fighting to hold back tears. He started to say something, but Pat yelled, "Go, Stickman!" The older boy rammed this palm between Greg's shoulder blades, shoving him toward the grove.

The thin boy stumbled forward, pausing once to look back. But instead of mercy, he just got a volley of "Go! Go! Go!" as the others waved him on.

He began running through the trees.

"Other end!" Pat ordered. Laughing, the four ran along the edge of the grove of trees; in their excitement they yelled and slammed fists into palms, crying, "Yes!"

In the thicket, Greg stumbled forward. What moonlight made its way through the leaves and branches barely let him see the path. Roots tripped him. Twigs and branches clawed at his face and arms and at his legs below his cutoffs. It was easy to imagine that spindly-armed creatures were grabbing at him. He thought of the scratches on Pat's arm. The tears that he had held back began to flow. He whimpered in fright but kept going—too afraid to look behind. The shadows ahead were scary enough. He let the air dry his tears, as he kept his arms pumping to keep up the pace.

He was sure he heard voices whispering in the green-black spaces around him; a bunch of leaves looked exactly like a face staring at him from high up in a tree. Then he lurched into the round, open dead zone that marked the halfway point. His toe caught on a stone, and he sprawled onto the ground. His glasses went flying. Without them, he was half blind. On his hands and knees, he groped around, but couldn't locate his glasses.

He was still searching the snarls of crab grass when he heard a loud crackling, like someone or something pushing through the trees. The whispers were now much louder and nearer. They weren't words, just soft sounds, like leaves brushed by the wind. For a moment he hoped his friends had followed him to tease him. Then, far away, beyond the blurry shadows of tangled trees and bushes, he heard them calling, "Hey, Stickman! Lose your way? Lose your nerve? Wet your pants?" Their insults and laughs, sifting through the wall of growing things, reminded him how alone he was.

He gave up the search for his glasses and stood up. At the same moment, something vast and green with a mouth like a black slit and eyes that were ragged, gaping holes appeared at one side of the clearing, near the path

he had just followed. Greg was glad that he couldn't see clearly whatever it was. Hardly daring to breathe, he backed to the opposite side of the clearing, guessed where the path continued, and started running. But he had guessed wrong. He blundered into a tangle of growing things that snared him.

He heard the rustling move closer to him. He tried to pull free, but something—a tree branch? an arm?—caught his hair and hooked his shirt collar. He threw himself to one side. A branch snapped, then he broke free. A second later, twigs like fingers scratched his forehead and cheek, drawing blood, then marking his skin with something sticky like sap. There was soft laughter in the velvet green darkness all around him. Then he found the path, and he ran from the green horror. The sap on his face burned at first, but then it seeped into his cuts and scratches. As it did so, it began to spread a comforting warmth all through him. He kept running, but the world was changing with each step—and so was he. The woods no longer felt scary; his legs and arms were no longer rubbery with fear; the laughter of his former friends—closer now—no longer hurt. He ran eagerly toward the mocking voices just ahead.

At the far end of the zigzag path, Pat was leading the others in shouting insults and laughing. But he was beginning to get worried. What if the Stickman had tripped and broken his leg or run into a low-hanging tree branch and knocked himself out? First of all, they'd have to go in to look for him, and that was something none of them wanted. And, if the younger boy was hurt, it meant trouble for all of them.

So he breathed a sigh of relief when he heard the crackling and rustling as the Stickman pushed through the last trees and bushes. Just a few more yards, a few more feet . . .

The last greenery parted. But what came charging at Pat, who was closest, was a nightmare thing of brush and branches that grabbed the boy with wooden claws. It pushed a green face into his; but when it tried to talk, all that came out of the dark mouth hole was a gush of sap that blinded Pat and filled his mouth and throat—caught in mid-yell—with green heat.

Space Is the Place

There had been strange white lights in the sky for days. Sometimes there was just a single one; sometimes groups of lights flew in circles or Vs; more often they formed strange patterns like the pictures of crop circles Mark had seen in checkout stand magazines in the supermarket. People speculated excitedly on the cause, wrote to the newspapers, were interviewed on local television stations. Shaman's Spring was abuzz with talk of flying saucers, alien invasions, and glowing shapes glimpsed in the woods late at night. Of course, no one had really encountered an alien. But the fear and excitement remained at fever pitch; the chatter never died.

And, every night, there were those haunting lights in the skies.

"I don't like this one bit," Mark's mother, Sherri, said. "I feel so isolated here." She and Mark had moved to the little North Carolina town of Shaman's Spring the year before, just after Mark's father was killed in a car crash. Sherri Mixon had opened an art gallery to sell paintings to summer visitors, but the business wasn't doing very well. She had already been talking of selling it and moving back to Asheville, before the light show in the skies began. At first, the idea of moving back suited Mark. His friends were back in the city. He found the little mountain town a zero, home to dullards and doofuses.

But the place had definitely become more interesting with the arrival of the mysterious night lights. Those who read or watched a lot of science fiction—and Shaman's Spring seemed to have plenty of them—talked matter-of-factly about UFOs and motherships hiding behind cloud covers. They rattled on endlessly about aliens they called "grays" or those that looked like praying mantises or lizards. That kind of alien seemed interesting to Mark. He wasn't excited about the ones that other people said looked like tall, good-looking men and women, with lots of blond hair and *Star Trek* kinds of outfits. They sounded pretty ordinary. But to Mark, at age nine, any chance to meet real aliens was promising—even if they looked no scarier than Anakin Skywalker or the current captain of the starship *Enterprise*.

Of course, Mark had seen enough movies to know there was always the risk of meeting a nasty something that wanted to zap you or put you in a cage or chow down on you, but he trusted that he could spot a mean one in time to save himself and his mother. He started making a list of ways to get rid of monsters he'd seen in movies: salt water melted triffids; flamethrowers reduced a variety of creatures to toast; super lasers worked well. Germs got rid of Martians in *War of the Worlds*. That was easy—just sneeze or spit—a lot simpler than finding flamethrowers or laser generators.

His hopes of meeting any aliens—friendly or hostile—were crushed when his mother announced, "I want to get away from here for a while. I'll feel safer. I don't believe one word of that talk about bug-eyed monsters spying on the Baptist Church Spaghetti Dinner or big lizardy things scaring the Millers' chickens so they won't lay. But this town is going loony tunes. So we're going to stay with Grandma down in Asheville."

"But, Mom," he argued. "If there really *are* aliens, I'll miss my chance to see them."

"Don't be silly. I read that scientists are saying those lights are just ball lightning or swamp gas or something. But maybe it's radioactive. Or maybe it can hurt you like they say happens when you live too close to power lines. We're going, and that's that. Besides," she sighed, "it's not as if I'll lose much business. I've only had lookers in the gallery twice."

They would leave the next day, Friday, on the morning bus to Asheville. "I just don't trust that old car to get us all the way there and back," his mother said.

"Oh, man," said Mark. First no aliens, now dreaded hours on the bus. He'd stare out the window, his mother would read a book, and there would only be rest stops for a Coke or a hamburger to break the monotony.

His unhappiness grew that night as the strange lights put on their best show ever. Dark clouds, heavy with unfallen rain, hung over the mountain peaks the locals called the Three Wizards, because they looked like ancient men wearing tall, pointed caps. Red-gold fire seemed to burn deep inside the clouds, while swarms of blue and silver lights—in the strangest formations yet—flickered around them or disappeared into the fiery billows.

"Are you packing?" his mother called from her room. "We're gonna leave first thing."

"Yes, ma'am," he answered, never taking his elbows off the windowsill or his eyes off the amazing display. Suddenly, a dozen of the blue and silver lights darted down into the forest that lay between the town and the mountain slopes. They didn't reappear. Mark was more frustrated than ever to think that he wouldn't be able to go into the woods tomorrow and look for a spot where some of those glowing balls touched down. He imagined finding a burned spot on the forest floor, with maybe meteors or crystals or actual flying saucers at its center. Someone else would find something wonderful; someone else would be the first to meet an alien; Mark would see it on Grandma's chintzy 19-inch TV in Asheville. He banged his fist on the sill in disappointment.

The sound alerted his mother. When he heard her footsteps in the hall as she came to check on him, he tossed his knapsack on the bed and grabbed a pile of socks and underwear out of the drawer and threw these alongside.

"Is this all you've packed?" Sherri asked her son. "Let me help."

By the time they were finished, the rain had arrived, hiding the Three Wizards and the light show above them. Mark fell asleep to the steady drumming of rain against his windows, dreaming of the spaceships that were even now cooling in the night and of the creatures beginning to stir.

The bus station was crowded the next morning. The rain had slacked off but was still falling when his mother purchased their tickets. All anyone wanted to talk about was the lights the night before; like Mark's mother, they wanted to get away before "all hell broke loose."

Mark slurped a Coke while his mother sipped coffee. Through the rain-blurred windows, he watched for the appearance of the beat-up old Mountain Passage bus that would shake, rattle, and eventually roll them into Asheville.

The bus was late this morning. More and more people were looking from their wristwatches to the big clock on the station wall and shaking their heads. The Mountain Passage buses were always late, but this was worse than usual. When the bus was more than an hour overdue on the road that wound through the mountains and down to the lowlands, Mark's mother said, "Go ask the lady at the ticket counter if she has any idea where the bus is. It's gonna be after dark by the time we get to Grandma's."

The boy was unhappy about putting down his *X-Men* comic, but he did as he was told.

"Hon, if I had a clue, I'd tell you," said the woman at the counter. "They were due in from Crestline ages ago. The driver should have radioed in if he was runnin' late. But you know how those old buses are. Things work or they don't. And the rain never helps. All I can say is, he'll be here when he gets here."

Mark gave the news to his mother. She looked angry. "I don't like us going down the mountain when it's getting dark."

"Can we stay, then?" said Mark, thinking of searching for alien starships.

"No," she said. "Grandma's expecting us. I swear this bus line—"

But whatever she was going to tell him about Mountain Passage was forgotten as their bus finally pulled up under the overhanging station roof. Passengers grabbed for luggage, food, blankets—whatever they were taking. Mark had his knapsack and a bag of snacks; his mother had her suitcase, her purse, and a tote bag full of paperback romance novels and other things.

The bus was brand-new. Mark often saw the buses running up and down Main Street, but he had never seen a new one. This looked fresh out of the package, with silver-gray stripes and chrome shining everywhere. The windows, tinted blue, had no scratches or graffiti. On the side, the cartoon of a bus roaring over mountains looked freshly painted. To his mother's delight, the inside of the bus and the restroom at the back (she always checked that out first) were just as shiny-new.

"We'll be late," she said, "but we'll be comfortable."

The driver who took their tickets and helped store their luggage in an overhead bin looked shiny-new himself. He had on a crisp gray uniform, the silver badge on his cap gleamed, and his smile was so big it looked like it was freshly painted on. He was handsome, too; he gave Sherri a friendly wink when he took her ticket. Mark saw his mother go all red and embarrassed. But she looked pleased, even so.

The driver sat in a special booth near the front. It was different from any that Mark had seen: it had frosted glass around it, so you could see only the driver's blurry shape when he was sitting with the narrow door closed. "It's for security," he explained, when Mark asked him about it.

The bus was almost completely full. Mark and his mother took seats halfway back. Mark got the window. "I am sorry for the delay," the driver apologized. "There was something going on up by Skilling Run. The sheriff's car and two state trooper vehicles were parked beside the road. I think they were looking for something in the woods, but they would not tell us anything. They just held our bus for a while, then waved us through."

Aliens! thought Mark. He imagined the lawmen pushing through the dripping branches, suddenly being zapped or swallowed or met by an outer-space person in silver spandex saying, "We come in peace." And he was missing it all!

The rain was coming down heavily as they pulled out of town. Looking back, Mark could just barely see the Three Wizards through the rain. Here and there around the mountain he saw flashes, but he couldn't tell if it was plain old lightning or what some people were calling "spook lights."

"Goodbye, aliens," he muttered. Goodbye, too, to his chance for adventure.

The bus rolled beyond the town, and trees pressed in on either side. This was the worst part of the trip for Mark: just trees, trees, trees, and the first rest stop over two hours down the road.

"Hey, these windows don't open," someone complained from the back of the bus.

"The vehicle is air-conditioned and heated for your comfort," said the driver's voice through the loudspeaker above his booth. "The restroom has been sanitized for your safety."

"Nice," murmured Sherri, never looking up from her book.

Mark gave his attention to the GameBoy he had gotten from his grandmother on his last birthday. He hoped to talk her into some new games while he was in Asheville. His mother wouldn't let him buy Resident Evil or The Thing, but Grandma could be persuaded, if they went shopping without his mother riding shotgun.

A few people chatted in whispers; most settled back into their seats and snoozed. Trees rolled by endlessly as the bus sped smoothly down the road and sailed easily around curves. Then the driver did a curious thing, turning

off onto a side road that wound over to the little town of Pickford before circling back to the main road. No bus that Mark had ridden on had ever gone this way.

He climbed over his mother, who hardly looked up from her paperback as she shifted to let him pass, thinking he was on a bathroom break. But Mark went and tapped on the driver's door.

"Yes?" came the driver's voice from the loudspeaker. He didn't offer to open the door or roll down the frosted-glass window.

"How come we're going this way?" Mark asked.

"The route has been changed," the voice answered. "We have a new stop."

"But we'll miss the Burger King," Mark said.

"We will stop soon. Be patient. Let me drive the bus."

Mark pressed his face so close to the glass that his nose left a spot. The driver paid no attention. He was just a blur. But, up close, Mark could see his hands as they turned the steering wheel or touched the lighted red, green, or gold buttons on the dashboard. The boy was impressed at how much more complicated new buses were.

He tapped on the glass. "Can I look inside for a minute?"

The driver continued to ignore him. Mark tapped louder and asked again. This time the driver said, "I am not supposed to answer unnecessary questions. Please return to your seat."

Mark did, thinking of a hamburger and wondering where the driver planned to stop. There was no fast-food stand in Pickford. He'd gone to the town with his mother months before when she had picked up some paintings from an artist who lived there. There was only a grocery sold sandwiches, he thought, so they'd stop there.

But they didn't stop in Pickford. They sped right through town. A mile or two beyond, the driver turned off the Pickford paved road onto a gravel road. Now everybody on the bus was awake and wondering what was going on. Two men were banging on the driver's booth, but the gray shape behind the frosted glass ignored them.

The men began to shout. To Mark they sounded scared and angry at the same time. Pretty soon everybody on the bus was yelling except Mark. He was enjoying the excitement and tension of the unexpected.

The bus rolled faster down the unused road, flinging gravel every which way.

Mark's mother was talking to the woman across the aisle. The two were frantically waving their hands.

"Do you think we're being hijacked?" asked Mark, making his way up the aisle slowly, as the bus bounced and jounced along the side road. This promised to be a better adventure than looking for aliens. Only, saving his mother and the other passengers was going to be more difficult, he thought. Spitting or sneezing on a hijacker would only make him angry—germs wouldn't kill him. But Mark was sure he could come up with a plan that would turn him into a hero who saved the day for everyone.

"There is no cause for alarm," the driver's voice said, as the men pounded on his booth. "We are right on schedule."

This only made the passengers babble more loudly. One man was trying to punch through the glass on the booth, but all he did was hurt his hand.

Mark had heard stories of bus drivers going whacko. There'd been one who'd driven off with a bunch of school kids, and another who'd kidnapped a church choir.

Around a turn in the road, Mark saw a grassy meadow. It was puddled with rain.

"There is no cause for alarm," the driver repeated. "This vehicle has been pressurized for your comfort and safety. Earth-normal gravity will be maintained. You should experience no distress."

They were no longer rolling across the grass now. The bus was angling into the air like a departing plane. People were screaming and crying and whimpering all at once. Hands beat uselessly against windows and against the cubicle where the driver (or was he the pilot?) sat.

"Oh, my sweet—!" Mark's mother gasped, fingers digging into her son's arm.

"Awesome!" breathed Mark as he saw the mothership slide from the cloud bank overhead. An *alien* hijacking. Now here was adventure—and his chance to be a hero. But there would be time enough for heroics later, he thought. Right now, he watched fascinated as a port in the mothership gaped open to swallow their airborne bus.

Ants

It's the *Disney* movie at MovieMax," Kyle explained to his mother for the twentieth time. Because her back was to him as she lifted a pitcher down from a kitchen cabinet, she didn't see him throw up his hands and make a face to indicate just how dense adults could be.

"*Which* Disney movie?" his mother asked, turning to look at him.

Kyle had done his homework. He correctly told her the name of the film, what it was about, even the starting time.

"Who else is going?" she asked.

"Just Stefan. His brother Craig works there, so he can get us in for free."

"That's nice," said his mother. Kyle knew that she was thinking: *Stefan's mother is even stricter than I am, so it must be okay.*

"I want you home *on time*," his mother said finally.

"I know. Five o'clock."

"—and not one minute later," they said together. For a minute he was afraid she was going to ground him for making fun. But she just shook her head and said, "Enjoy the movie. Be careful."

But Kyle was already slamming the kitchen door behind him.

Stefan was waiting for him at the corner. They raced each other to the mall, six blocks away, winding up in a dead heat. At the MovieMax complex, Stefan's brother, who was taking tickets, slipped them into the theater showing *Jungle Jaws of Death*. For days Kyle and Stefan had looked forward to the horror film, which the newspaper ads described as "Killer ants on the march. Nothing stands in their way. It's *their* party, and *you're* their picnic."

Previews of coming attractions were beginning as they slid into seats near the front. The first films previewed looked stupid, the boys agreed, but the preview for *Frightmaster* looked really scary. "He has the power to make your worst fears come true," a booming voice promised. "Your nightmares become reality." As loud music pounded away, a red-cloaked figure with a wide-brimmed red hat pulled low, showing only his staring eyes, filled the screen. "His victims are destroyed by their nightmares come true." The Frightmaster was gone. Now the boys saw teenagers chased by someone in a Halloween mask, people terrified by zombies, a screaming woman grabbed by something horrible jumping out of a closet.

The boys jumped too. "Cool!" they agreed. As the screen faded to black, the thunderous voice warned, "Keep repeating, *It's all in my mind. Frightmaster.* Coming soon to this theater."

The feature began. In a South American jungle, a team of scientists search for the legendary *marabunda*—killer ants fifty times more deadly than the fearsome army ants. They find the remains of animals, their bones picked clean. A dugout canoe drifts to shore with what seems to be a man asleep under a sombrero, but when one scientist lifts the hat, a skull grins up at them. The first killer ant crawls out of an eyehole. ("Gross!" whispered Kyle. "Yeah!" Stefan agreed happily.) The scientists take the ant to their camp to study it, but she sends a signal to her fellows, who come swarming in. Surrounded by *marabunda,* the scientists take shelter in an old mission. Ants finish off several people, including the old padre at the mission. At the last minute the others are saved when the hero, covered with ants but struggling on, dynamites a dam, drowns the ants, and manages to survive and save his girlfriend and everyone else. End of movie, except for a last shot of a surviving queen ant and the promise of *Jungle Jaws of Death, Part II.*

The boys stayed to watch the movie a second time, sitting again through the previews. Again the *Frightmaster* preview warned them, *"It's all in my mind."* Then they were watching the killer ants again. By the time it was over, Kyle realized he would have to hurry to be home on time. Leaving Stefan to go home with his brother, he raced back.

But as he ran, scenes from the movie kept replaying in his head. The first ant crawling out of a skull. Ants swarming over the old padre at the mission. Especially the hero covered in clicking *marabunda*. Kyle found himself scratching his stomach, brushing his shoulder, as if ants were crawling on him. Of course, he was only imagining it. "You have too much imagination," his mother often told him. *It's all in my mind,* he tried to convince himself—but this only reminded him of the preview of the movie about people who were chased by things that had crawled out of their dreams and imaginations. He brushed away more imaginary ants.

As soon as he got home, he made a dash for the bathroom, ignoring his mother's question, "How was the movie?"

He pulled up his shirt and unfastened his jeans. He twisted and turned, checking himself from every angle in the mirror to be sure nothing was crawling on him. Then, mad at himself for being such a baby, he went in to watch TV until dinner.

"Did you enjoy the movie?" his mother asked again.

"It was stupid," he said, now almost wishing he *had* gone to the Disney movie. He continued to feel little whisks and tickles like tiny feet crawling, or tiny feelers brushing his skin, just under his tee shirt and socks. He double-checked.

Nothing. But when he tried to ignore the sensations, he couldn't. He kept scratching and brushing at the nothing.

At dinner, he continued to fidget, until his father said, "What's the matter? Ants in the pants?"

Kyle made an effort to sit still, since there was no way to explain what was happening without getting himself and his friends in big trouble for going to an R-rated movie. Not scratching was a misery. And there seemed to be no way for him to take his mind off ants. A few spilled poppy seeds from the dinner rolls seemed to move if he stared at them too long. The pepper his father dusted across the gravy on his mashed potatoes reminded Kyle of drowned ants floating in muddy water. Dessert was homemade cake with white frosting and strawberries on top, and strawberry jam between the layers. As his mother served the cake, she said, "When I was a little girl, I went with my mother to visit my great-grandmother. The poor old thing could hardly see. Well, she served us tea and crackers spread with strawberry jam. But there were as many ants as seeds in the jam. When I tried to say something, my mother shook her head and ate a cracker. She didn't want to hurt great-grandmother's feelings."

"What did you do?" asked Kyle, fascinated and grossed out.

"I ate mine and asked for a second one, to be polite," she said with a laugh. "But it wasn't till I was in college that I tried strawberry jam again."

While his parents chuckled at the story, Kyle carefully picked at his cake, avoiding the whole strawberries or any bit of jam filling.

Later Kyle brushed his teeth, said goodnight, and carefully shut his bedroom door. Then he laid his jacket across the bottom of the door so no light would seep out.

He planned to keep his lights on all night. He peeled back the blankets from his bed and sat crossed-legged on the white sheet. No ants could sneak up on him now.

Soon he heard the door to his parents' room shut, and the house settled into its late-night hush. He listened to the dark outside his closed window. He was sure he heard a clicking that wasn't made by crickets. He kept his eye on the window, where moths, attracted by the light, made soft patting sounds. The seconds and minutes on the digital clock seemed to advance more and more slowly.

He closed his eyes for a minute to rest them. Instantly he was running through a dream-jungle, while behind him came swarms of red *marabunda*, their jaws opening-shutting with awful clicks. Ahead he saw a mission like the one in the movie. But the Frightmaster, wrapped in red, was sitting on the steps, waiting. Kyle paused, caught between the ants and the nightmare figure. But the Frightmaster just laughed and said, "Hey, kid—it's only a dream. And dreams are all in your mind. What's to be afraid of?"

"Them!" cried Kyle, pointing behind. The jungle was alive with the deadly clicking of the red swarms.

"You'd better hole up inside," said the Frightmaster. He bowed, as if the boy was a visiting king, and took off his hat. His head was a skull. Then he vanished.

Kyle ran to the mission gates and pushed them open. Inside, the place was a mass of *marabunda*, hiding the ground, hanging like living curtains rippling along the walls. He turned back, but other ants were pouring out of

the jungle like a red river. Trapped, dream-Kyle screamed. Awakening with a grunt, Kyle found himself lying in his bed, the covers pulled up to his chin. Somehow he had rearranged the bed while he was asleep, tucking his dreaming self under the bedclothes. The clock showed that an hour had passed. Even under the warm blankets, he was shivering partly with cold and partly from his nightmare. Then he noticed that the crickets were silent; there were no moths at the window. And the window was open to the night air. Had he done that in his sleep, too? Staring at the window, he was unnerved by the deep, lifeless silence outside. "The *marabunda* eat *everything,*" someone had said in the movie earlier.

Something tweaked him on the leg. Again. Now there were pinpricks up and down both legs, on his arms, on his stomach underneath his pajama top. With a cry, he threw off the covers. The bed was a mass of red ants. He grabbed his pillow to bat them away, but the pillow deflated like a popped balloon, pouring *marabunda* down his neck and pajama sleeves. "They're just figments of your imagination, like me," said the Frightmaster deep inside Kyle's head. "But, then, you always *did* have too much imagination." He began to laugh.

Kyle, drowning like Pharaoh's army in his own red-sea bed, thought the laughter was definitely *uncool*. Then he stopped thinking altogether.

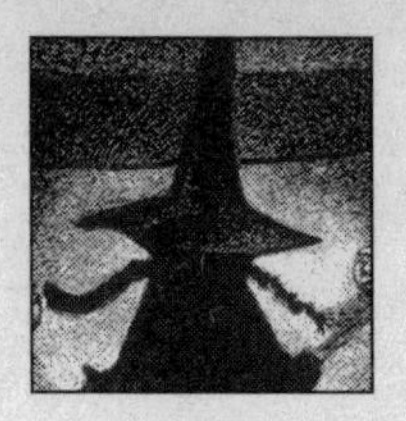

The Halloween Spirit

Keesha looked through the front window. The sky was still light, but already lots of kids were out on the street trick-or-treating. Their costumes were funny or scary or dumb. She recognized her friend Jamal. He had taken off the head of his outfit and was holding the foil-covered box decorated with twisted wire coathangers in one hand, and wiping his forehead with the other hand. Keesha guessed it was pretty hot inside the box, which only had two little eyeholes and earholes in it. She put a hand up to her mouth and laughed. Just what was he supposed to be? she wondered. A robot? A spaceman? A walking computer? He had clearly made his costume by himself. Two more boxes made up the body, and he'd wrapped more aluminum foil around his arms and legs. She was glad she didn't have to go trick-or-treating with anyone who looked that stupid.

She turned to look at herself in the hall mirror. Her mom had made her an Egyptian princess costume. She looked like Cleopatra, with a gold-painted headdress, lots of her mother's bracelets and necklaces, and skirts made of heavy blue-and-gold material that had cost more than her mother had planned to spend. But it was what Keesha wanted, and what Keesha wanted, she usually got.

Usually. Tonight her mother was insisting on something the girl *didn't* want *at all*. She was supposed to take her little sister, Jonelle, trick-or-treating. Keesha had whined and stamped her foot and argued that none of her other friends had to take a little sister or brother out with them, but her mother wouldn't listen.

"Isn't she ready yet?" she yelled down the hall to Jonelle's bedroom, where their mother was fixing the last of her younger daughter's costume. "We'll miss all the good stuff."

"Hush!" her mother answered. "You won't miss anything." A minute later, she announced, "There. We're all set."

She came down the hall, leading five-year-old Jonelle by the hand. The child was dressed as a witch in a store-bought costume she had picked out for herself. Her mother had had to shorten the black skirts a bit, because Jonelle was so small. She had her plastic witch mask pulled down. The green, warty skin; long, crooked nose; scraggly yellow teeth; and clip-on, green-tipped fingernails were so "been there, done that" Keesha could barely stand it. The pointed plastic cap had some fake gray curls sewn to it, hiding Jonelle's cornrows interwoven with bright colored beads. She was carrying a plastic broom in one hand. In the other was a papier-mâché pumpkin to hold her Halloween treats.

Keesha felt fresh anger at her sister and mother. She tried one last time, "Mama, it's not *fair* to make me take her."

Her mother held up her hand. "That's the end of it. You'll do as you're told, or you're not going out at all."

"Come on," Keesha said, grabbing Jonelle's hand roughly.

"Ow! Mama, make her stop!" Jonelle pulled away.

"Keesha!" The girl got the message in that one word. With a sigh, she took Jonelle's hand extra gently.

"Don't either of you eat anything until you get home. I want a close look at what you got before you take a taste."

"Yes, Mama," said Keesha.

"And stay out of the park. Those big kids get up to mischief there."

"I know, Mama," said Keesha. The park was *exactly* where she intended to go sooner or later. As soon as she got rid of the tag-along who'd surely tattle.

They went first to a few close-by houses. Even though her sister was smaller, Keesha felt that Jonelle was deliberately walking slowly. It took them forever to reach each front door, while other groups of kids hurried up and down and moved on to the next house. At this rate, Keesha figured, she was going to get the least Halloween treats ever. And people fussed over the little girl in her Rite-Aid outfit, hardly noticing Keesha's costume.

"Walk faster!" she ordered, giving Jonelle's arm a sharp tug.

"*Ow!* I'm telling!"

"Mama's not here. Be quiet! You really are a little *witch*, you brat!"

"Mama told you to be nice," said Jonelle. She sounded ready to cry under her witch's mask.

A ghost, skeleton, devil, and mummy passed them, laughing as they headed up the street. "Hey, Keesha, you look good!" said the ghost in her friend M'shell's voice. "Comin' to the park?"

"Not yet. I gotta take care of *this* miserable little witch."

"Too bad," said M'shell. The four ran off in the direction of the park.

"You're spoiling everything," Keesha snarled.

Now Jonelle really did begin crying.

"Hey, I'm sorry," said Keesha. She really wasn't, but she knew if Jonelle got going, there'd be no stopping her tears. She lifted the mask, dried her sister's tears, and put the mask back. By the time they'd poked along to two more doors, Keesha realized that only little kids in costumes and their parents were out. All the kids her own age had vanished—probably to the park.

She made her mind up. She'd get in trouble, but she was going too.

"Come on," she insisted, half dragging a protesting Jonelle along. "We're going to the park."

"Mama said no. And it scares me."

"It'll be cool. All my friends are there. You'll have fun."

"Mama said no."

"Look, I'll give you half my candy if you'll go."

"I don't *want* any more candy. And Mama said, *No*."

"Well I say, *Yes!*" She gave Jonelle's arm the hardest yank she could.

The girl wailed like she was being killed. Keesha ignored her, marching along, and never letting go. Jonelle had to run on her short legs to keep up.

They had just reached the edge of the city park when Jonelle broke free and started running for home. "I'm telling, I'm telling, I'm *telling!*" she screeched. Keesha tried to follow, but her sandal caught in the hem of her Egyptian skirts. Down she went onto the lawn, as Jonelle rounded the corner and disappeared down their street.

Keesha climbed to her feet. There were wet grass stains down one side of her skirt. Her headdress had fallen off, and one side was pushed in.

"Run on home, you little witch," she called after her long-gone sister.

Trying to straighten her headdress, she stomped into the park, looking for her friends.

It was a pleased Keesha who found them in the hollow, spider-webbed space under the old-fashioned band shell where groups played music in summer. Here they'd be hidden from the eyes of parents or police. Some of the older kids had beer and cigarettes and stuff. Keesha was too smart to mess with any of *that:* she was already in big trouble, she was sure. Well, she told herself, she'd deal with Jonelle and her mama later. After all, it was Jonelle's word against her own. She could get one of her friends to back her up. They'd say Jonelle ran off and Keesha looked everywhere for her. The idea of avoiding trouble and maybe getting Jonelle grounded cheered her.

Her best friends were clustered around a bunch of red, white, and black candles. Cassandra, whose grandmother had come from New Orleans, and who believed in all kinds of magic, had taken some of the old woman's "Hoodoo." She was busily lighting the candles.

"What's *she* up to now?" asked Keesha, sitting down near M'shell. She hated Cassie, who was always cool and was the one their friends accepted as natural leader of the group. That was a role Keesha wanted but never won.

"Cassie's gonna conjure up a monster for us," M'shell whispered back. She rolled her eyes as if to say, *Oh, yeah, sure!*

"Shouldn't mess with that kind of stuff," Jamal said uneasily.

"It never works," said M'shell. "But it's fun to pretend."

Following Cassie's directions, ten of them sat in twos, each pair at one point of a five-pointed star—Cassie called it a pentagram—she had drawn in chalk on the poured concrete flooring. Cassie knelt in the middle, waving her hands over the lit candles in front of her. Keesha and M'shell, one of the pairs, got a case of the giggles, barely stopping before Cassie could order them out.

"I summon the nearest spirit of Halloween," said Cassie.

Everyone else began to chant, "Appear! Appear! Appear!" as Cassie had told them to. Feeling silly, Keesha joined in. She avoided looking at M'shell, sure they'd both start laughing again.

The chanting grew louder. The older kids began to laugh at them, then warned them to quiet down before the cops came to bust them all.

"I feel a spirit," said Cassie, who seemed to be caught up in her own mumbo jumbo. She made her voice so deep that for a minute Keesha half believed a spirit had taken over her friend's body. Like in *The Exorcist*. Then M'shell wrinkled her nose in a way that gave Keesha the giggles.

"QUIET!" Cassie yelled so loudly she startled even the older kids into silence. She continued in the strange, deep voice, "The spirits are here to share their power. If you laugh at them, they'll put a curse on you. Make your peace with them, and you'll get a wish."

Tired of seeing Cassie at center stage, Keesha said, "Yeah, well, if there were spirits, and not just you pretending, I'd have them make *pieces* of my little sister, who's always making trouble for me." She began to laugh at her own bad joke. M'shell and a few others joined in weakly, as if they might be believing what Cassie said.

"A wish for evil is often turned back on the wisher," Cassie warned. "The spirits play a dangerous game."

"Well, this game is over 'cause I don't want to play anymore," Keesha announced. She stood up suddenly.

"Don't open the pentagram!" screeched Cassie.

"Get over the game, girl," sneered Keesha. "Your spirits are nothing and neither are you."

There was a sudden flash of blue as all the candles flared at once.

"Who farted?" yelled Jamal, falling backward in a pretend faint. The pentagram dissolved into laughter.

"Idiots!" said Cassie, pinching out her grandmother's candles.

"Hey! We did get a spirit after all," said M'shell, "Only, it's kind of a puny one." Everyone looked to where she was pointing.

Jonelle, in her green witch mask, was standing just inside the enclosed space. She had her toy broom and her pumpkin of candy, and she was staring at her sister.

"Oh, man," groaned Keesha. "I am gonna be *so busted* when the brat tells Mama what's going on here." She knew the younger girl would be sure to talk about the beer and stuff the older kids had brought.

"Give her your candy, or tell her you'll knock her into next Halloween," M'shell suggested.

"She doesn't want more candy, and the little witch knows I won't hit her."

"Maybe you can sweet-talk her."

"Maybe. But I bet I'm grounded for a month." Keesha got to her feet and dusted off her costume. It was as big a mess as her whole night had become.

She held out her hand to her sister. Jonelle took it. Her hand felt cold. "You're not sick, are you? 'Cause if you are, I'll get blamed for that, too."

Jonelle shrugged. She followed silently, tugged along by her big sister.

Halfway across the park, Keesha said, "Aren't you hot in that mask?"

Jonelle shook her head.

"Whatever. You gonna tell Mama what happened tonight? Where I've been?"

Jonelle nodded.

"*Witch!* How about if I give you half my allowance? No—*all* of it? You still gonna tell?"

Another nod.

Keesha jerked her sister's arm angrily. The girl hissed in surprise. Keesha hoped it had *really* hurt her.

"Why did you come back? To spy on me?"

Jonelle said nothing.

"Why don't you talk, little witch?" She jerked the arm again and got an answering gasp that she was sure meant pain. She let go of the other's still-freezing hand. She grabbed the papier-mâché pumpkin and emptied it into her own bag. "Might as well get something out of this night," she said.

Jonelle tagged along quietly. Keesha dropped the empty pumpkin after a few steps. "You like this, don't you?" she asked. She nudged the jack-o'-lantern with her toe.

Jonelle nodded.

"Too bad," said her sister, who felt anger bursting out in every direction, like the points on Cassie's pentagram. She slammed her foot down three or four times, flattening the pumpkin to an orange-yellow wad. "Your pumpkin, my Halloween—they're both wrecked now."

They were out of the park now, and she was rushing her sister so that the little girl tripped twice. Each time, the plastic broom clacked on the sidewalk. Keesha yanked Jonelle to her feet as roughly as she could. She was surprised that the other didn't yell or burst into tears. She just took it, which wasn't like Jonelle at all. Maybe she was sick, Keesha thought, feeling guilty for a minute—but only a minute.

Around the corner, and there was their house. "Here comes trouble," Keesha muttered. *"Big time."*

At their mailbox, Keesha looked up the path to the front door with the feeling a prisoner might have looking down the last mile to the electric chair.

As she started up the path, Jonelle suddenly got weird. She clamped her hand around Keesha's wrist, and hid behind the folds of her sister's costume. Her small hand felt tight as a handcuff.

They were almost to the front porch when the door opened, and light poured down the steps. Their mother appeared in the doorway. Jonelle was still hidden behind Keesha, holding onto her hand for dear life.

"Keesha!" her mother said, "Get yourself up here. You've got plenty of explaining to do."

Keesha took a step closer. Her right arm was still behind her, locked in Jonelle's grip. Why was her sister acting so crazy? she wondered. She expected the brat to be running to their mother with all sorts of tears and tattle.

"I'm sorry, Mama," she said.

"You *should* be, girl! Your sister coming home in tears and all. I've only just got her calmed down."

"What do you mean, Mama?" Keesha felt Jonelle's hold on her wrist tighten to the point of painfulness.

"Ask your sister, not me!"

Jonelle, munching an apple, appeared beside their mother. She was still wearing her witchy skirts, but she had taken off her mask and pointed hat. She had her green-tipped plastic nails wrapped around the apple like the witch in *Snow White*. "You were mean, Keesha," she said, sticking out her tongue.

Confused, Keesha spun around to face the Jonelle who had her in a wristlock. For a moment the two just stared at each other. Then the short masked figure began to grow and grow, the fingers that held Keesha turned strong as steel bands, and the mask was no mask, for the mouth was moving. "Happy Halloween!" cried the witch, who now towered nearly eight feet tall in her pointed cap. "You've caught the Halloween spirit, and it's caught you!" The toy broom had grown huge along with its mistress.

"Mama! Jonelle! Help!" Keesha begged.

But her mother was rooted in shock. Jonelle fled screaming into the house, her dropped apple bouncing down the steps. Their mother just gaped as the witch, skirts billowing, spiraled on her broom into the night sky, hauling Keesha along. Faster and faster they spun—witchy black and Egyptian gold in a blur, whirling like a tornado.

The Egyptian headdress hit the mailbox and rolled into the gutter. An instant later, pieces of the costume—and Keesha—followed like a soft, pattering rain.

The Bald Mountain Monster

Nick's adoptive parents, Carl and Maryjo Hopkins, were both herpetologists—which Nick would point out to his friends meant that they studied reptiles and amphibians. When that didn't cut it, he explained that herpetologists studied snakes, lizards, and salamanders. At this point, most of his friends got it. His parents taught at the University of Miami. Sometimes the university or someone else gave them money to go places and look for rare creatures.

This particular summer, the Doctors Hopkins had been granted funds to go on a camping trip to western North Carolina, where they hoped to find a rare ruby-striped tree frog. They agreed to take Nick and his friends

Angel Espinosa and Sarah Spencer on the weeklong camping trip. Sarah's mother, Noreen, went along. She was an artist who loved to paint animals and birds in their wilderness settings.

The group set up base camp on the lower slopes of one of the mysterious "mountain balds" in the area. "These mountaintops," Carl Hopkins explained as they unpacked the SUV and set up their tents, "are from 2,000 to 6,000 feet high. They don't have any trees or even bushes on them. No one knows why. Some think it has to do with the soil; some think the Indians cleared the peaks to use as lookouts. But the wooded area just below should be ideal for finding our tree frog."

The particular bald they had chosen to explore had the curious name Scoble Dome. On the second day, while Nick's folks went tree-frog hunting and Sarah's mother set up her easel to paint, the three youngsters went exploring. They were under strict orders to stay close together, stay on the path, and stay close to camp.

After hiking about half an hour, Nick, who was in front, said, "There's a cabin up ahead."

Sarah said, "It looks empty. Maybe it's one of those places hunters use."

Angel, who always took the more direct approach to things, went up and rapped on the door. It was opened by an old man, who seemed quite surprised to see the three friends. "Don't get many visitors," he said. "My name is Wesley Scoble." He invited them in to cool off, and they accepted. Though the outside of the cabin was weather-beaten, the inside was neat enough. Two walls of the main room were covered with bookshelves. Nick, who loved to read, couldn't help looking over the old man's collection. "You read a lot of history and science fiction," he said at last.

"Yep. I like to know what happened in the past, and I think of science fiction as the history of the future. I like knowing where we've been and where we might be headed."

Sarah said, "You have the same name as this mountain: Scoble. Did you name the place?"

"No. It's named for my great-times-three grandfather, who was an early settler in this area."

The children explained how they happened to be in the area. Then Nick said, "My dad says no one's sure why nothing grows here. Or on any of the mountain balds."

"Oh, there's probably a simple reason," said Wesley Scoble, "but I like the more fanciful ones. There's an old Indian legend about why nothing grows on this mountain. You interested?"

The three friends were. As Nick and Sarah perched on the old sofa and Angel sat on the rug, the old man settled into a rocking chair and began to talk. "Long before the first white people moved into the area," he said, "the local Indian tribes were terrified by a strange creature with leathery wings and sharp teeth and claws that would snatch children and carry them off to the mountaintop to eat. When the creature flew, its outstretched wings made a huge shadow on the ground. Bad luck was supposed to come to anyone touched by the shadow."

"Sounds like a pterodactyl," Nick interrupted. "One of those leather-winged dinosaurs that could fly—well, *glide,* really."

Wesley Scoble just shrugged and continued his story: "When the monster stole the son of one of the most powerful chiefs, the leader called together his own warriors and those of other tribes. The men bravely set out to battle the mountain horror, whose size, strength, and fierceness were only too well known.

"When they reached the heavily wooded top of the mountain, however, they found dozens of the birds there. The creatures had been asleep for hundreds of years, but now they were waking up. To destroy so many of the monsters, the Indians decided to set fire to the woods. The flames swept up the mountains, destroying everything. Then the Indians gave thanks to the Great Spirit. But nothing grew after the fire.

"There's a second legend," Wesley Scoble added, "that says a few young creatures hid in caves, went back to sleep, and will wake up some day. To keep this from happening, the Indians kept burning off the mountaintop to destroy any survivors. By the time the tribes died out, the grasses and shrubs were the only things left growing. No trees could get started. Scoble Dome was as bare in Grandfather Scoble's day as it is now."

Since it was getting late in the afternoon and they had a long trek back to camp, Nick, Sarah, and Angel soon said their goodbyes. But they promised to visit again before returning home.

That night, the three took turns telling the adults the legend.

"That's quite a story," said Carl Hopkins.

"It's interesting how people invent tales to explain purely natural things, isn't it?" said Nick's mother, Maryjo.

"Thank you, but I prefer deer and raccoons to giant man-eating birds," said Noreen Spencer, pretending to shiver.

"Wouldn't it be great if the story was true?" asked Nick. "Sort of like a real *Jurassic Park*."

That night, Nick and Angel, who shared one pup tent, talked long into the night about the possibility that a few of the ancient creatures had survived. At one point, Angel said, "Quiet! You hear that?"

"What?" asked Nick. But he listened.

"Wings," his friend whispered. "Great. Big. Wings. Coming close. Closer."

Nick strained to hear.

"Gotcha!" yelled Angel, grabbing Nick's shoulder, making his friend yell.

"Quiet, you two!" ordered Carl Hopkins from his tent. "We've got a busy day tomorrow."

But the boys kept talking in whispers about the possibility that something might still be alive in some deep cave on Scoble Dome.

In the morning, Maryjo Hopkins asked the youngsters to help search for the ruby-striped tree frog. They agreed, though all three would have preferred looking for a leather-winged dragon. Noreen Spencer stayed to work on her painting of hawks riding the air currents above the nearby slopes. As they climbed up through the thinning trees toward the bald part of the mountain, everyone was caught up in the excitement of the hunt for the rare frog. The stories of flying monsters were temporarily forgotten.

It was Nick who spotted one of the elusive frogs in the fork of a tree growing just off the trail. He was a little ahead of the others, so he moved his hand up and down to quiet their talk, then signaled to them to come closer. Carl had his camera out and aimed. Maryjo held Sarah and Angel back, not wanting to scare the tiny frog that hadn't taken its eyes off Nick.

Suddenly, a rock slid out from under Carl Hopkins's boot. The scientist gave a shout, dropping his camera as he slid down the steep slope. "Carl!" cried Maryjo. Nick spun around to look. The frog vanished in a flicker. Nick's father grabbed at bushes, but his slide ended as he slammed with a *whoompf!* into the stump of a lightning-blasted tree. He lay with the wind knocked out of him as his wife, ordering the kids to stay put, picked her way down to where he was.

"Is Dad okay?" asked Nick worriedly. Angel and Sarah stood on either side of him, watching just as anxiously.

"I think he's bruised a rib," his mother called back. "And he's twisted his ankle."

"It's my dignity that hurts the most," his father added, making a joke. But the rib and the ankle weren't jokes. It took the adults a long time to climb back to the path. Angel recovered the dropped camera. "Never even got a picture," said Carl a few minutes later, as he leaned on a tree branch he was using as a crutch. The adults got ready to head back to camp, where Maryjo had a first-aid kit.

"Give me your camera, Dad," said Nick. "We're going to go a little bit further up the trail. Maybe I'll spot another frog and get you your picture."

The adults went their way, after giving all the usual warnings to the kids. Nick, followed by Sarah and Angel, led the way. And luck was on Nick's side: he found a second tree frog, clinging to the side of a scrub pine. While Nick set up the camera tripod the way his father had taught him, his friends amused themselves by exploring the mountainside higher up, where trees no longer grew and the bald began.

Just as the camera went *clickclickclick,* Nick heard a shout from Angel. Nick quickly folded up the camera tripod and strapped it to his back. He hurried to where his friend stood beside a narrow opening—little more than a crack—in the rocky cliff. "Sarah's inside. She said she heard something like a weird bird call and went to look."

"That was stupid!" said Nick. "She could have crawled into a rattlesnake nest!"

"I heard her say she could see some light, then she yelled she was falling. I think I can hear her, but she sounds far away."

Nick stuck his head into the opening. "Sarah!" he shouted.

"Down here," she answered. "I'm all right, but I can't climb out. There's a little light. And I hear something, but I'm afraid to go look."

"Let me see," said Nick. To Angel he said, "If I'm not back in a couple of minutes, go tell my folks. They'll know what to do."

Without waiting, he squeezed through the opening. Inside, the passage widened, so that he could move along more easily. Just enough light filtered through the entrance to let him see what he was doing. From somewhere up ahead, Sarah called, "Nick. Angel. *Someone*."

"Hang on, I'm coming," Nick shouted back.

A short distance in, the tunnel ended in a shaft. The bottom was only a few feet straight down; but the top went up and up until it ended in a sliver of sunlight far above. In the shadows below, he could make out Sarah looking up at him.

"Be careful, the edge is—" Sarah warned.

But Nick had discovered the danger the hard way as the lip of the pit crumbled. He suddenly stood on nothing, dropping onto his butt, then riding a fall of dirt and stones down to the bottom. Dust blinded and choked him. More stones fell. He staggered to his feet, shaken, but with nothing broken. The pit was filled with choking dust. More stones and dirt were avalanching down. He stuck out his hands and felt Sarah grab one. She pulled him into a second narrow tunnel as more dirt and rocks *whooshed* into the pit. Like a blind man, he let his friend pull him away from the collapsed pit. He struggled to catch his breath, but he kept coughing up the dust that filled his nose and mouth and throat, though he kept his free hand over the lower part of his face.

He was aware that the tunnel had turned and turned again. Finally, the air grew cool and dust-free. Nick scraped the dust from his eyes. In a faint light, he saw Sarah slapping dust from her jacket and jeans. "Smooth move," she said. "You buried the way in."

"Hey! It wasn't me who went crawling into the dark to begin with."

They might have argued some more, but there was a faint cry, like something between a bird call and a kitten's mewl. "That's the sound I heard," whispered Sarah. "Now I don't think I want to know what it is."

"Well, we're gonna find out," said Nick. "There's some light coming from that end of the tunnel. And there's a breeze blowing from there. So that may be a way out. We're sure not going back the way we came."

The strange cry came again. Sarah put her fingers to her lips, then whispered, "Let's not make a sound until we know what's making that noise."

Nick nodded.

Holding hands, maintaining silence, they walked toward the grayish light ahead. Where the tunnel ended, they found themselves on a ledge halfway up the wall of a huge cavern. The ledge ran around one side of the cave, as though long ago the top half of the cave had moved slightly off its base, creating the ledge on one side and an overhang on the other. Light came through a number of smaller and bigger openings scattered up the sides. One was directly across from them, just inches above the far part of the ledge they were standing on.

"That may be a way out," Nick whispered in her ear. "Anyhow, it's our best bet."

"I don't know if I can make it," said Sarah, who had been keeping her palm pressed against the cave wall. "It looks so narrow and crumbly."

"We'll take it easy. Hug the wall if you need to. But there's no other way."

They heard the strange piping-mewling sound again. Much louder, it seemed to come from over their heads. They both stared up to where the rounded roof of the cave was hung with stalactites. As they watched, the biggest one suddenly shuddered, partly unfolded gray, leathery wings, cried once more, then settled down.

"It's one of the things Mr. Scoble told us about!" Nick said. "It's sleeping upside down like a bat up there. Maybe it's hibernating. I hope it doesn't wake up soon. I know how hungry I am after a night's sleep."

"Stop! You're scaring me," Sarah whispered.

"I'm scaring myself, too," Nick admitted.

High above, the creature stirred again.

"We go now!" the boy insisted. Sarah nodded; clearly her other fears were overcome by the danger of staying so near the creature. And going back was a dead end. So they moved slowly along the ledge, Nick leading. Both kept as close to the wall as possible, being careful to keep from crunching pebbles underfoot or kicking a stone off

the path. They were afraid that any noise might wake the sleeping monster.

They had almost reached the far opening, when a rock Nick was holding for support suddenly came loose. He yelled and started to pitch to the side; Sarah screamed, but grabbed him, steadied him, all the while praying that her own hold wouldn't fail. The loosened rock crashed and banged its way into the depths, adding its noise to the echoes of the kids' yells.

The creature overhead woke with a hiss that grew to a bloodcurdling screech. It unfolded its wings to the full. The head darted from side to side, up and down, searching for the source of the noise, spotting the kids instantly. The claws let loose of the stony perch. The monster dive-bombed toward them through the gloom.

"Hurry!" said Nick, scrambling the last few feet along the ledge. Sarah followed right behind. The boy stumbled into the tunnel entrance, sprawling full length when his foot caught on a rocky outcropping a few feet inside. Sarah tripped over him. For a moment they were so busy untangling themselves, they forgot the monstrous bird. Then they heard the creature's claws rake the side of the entrance. Its screech of disappointment at missing its prey filled the cavern.

"Are we safe?" asked Sarah.

"No way!" Nick answered, pulling her back just as the beak, its edges serrated like a saw, snapped shut an inch from her boot. The friends pushed and shoved each other down the tunnel, toward a faint splotch of light. Behind, the creature had found that, with its wings folded, it was able to squeeze batlike into the opening. Clearly, it wasn't about to let them go.

Now the tunnel was widening as it slanted upward toward what looked like daylight. Behind them, the monster inched forward. The beak snapped again and again. Its screeching was deafening in the narrow space that continued to widen. They were making better time, scrambling up the steepening slope, helping each other. But the creature was doing better, too. As the tunnel widened, it was able to use its wings more effectively to push itself along. It seemed able to navigate the limited space quite easily. Thoughts were tumbling through Nick's brain as they kept up their frantic climb. So much for all those movies where people save themselves from dinosaurs or whatever by ducking into a narrow space at the last possible moment. Now he was beginning to think that this might be the entrance the creature once used to go in and out of its cave when it went hunting in ages past.

Even if they beat it into the open air, Nick thought, it would follow them. And what chance would they have on the mountainside against such an airborne monster?

More snapping, more screeching. Then they were out in the sunshine. The mountainside dropped sharply away, with no hint of shelter.

On came the creature, looking more snakelike than ever.

"Throw rocks. Maybe that'll stop it."

He and Sarah began to throw the biggest stones they could find. This only seemed to make the monster angrier.

They tried to loosen several bigger stones, but these wouldn't budge. "I need a lever! Find a branch or something!" yelled Nick. But the treeless slope offered nothing.

"Your dad's camera!" cried Sarah.

The deadly beak was no more than twenty feet below them, as Nick unfastened the camera tripod. He jammed the three metal legs, folded together, under the most promising boulder. Working together, they dislodged the stone just as the tip of the deadly beak jutted into the air. The boulder connected, the beak disappeared, and the thing screamed in fury. In a minute, it was struggling back up, but Nick and Sarah, working smoothly as a team, sent one boulder after another down the shaft. Now some of the boulders were taking other stones and shale down too.

Not daring to stop, they circled the shaft mouth, prying loose every stone they could.

The screeching had grown weak. They couldn't tell if they were burying the creature or simply driving it back. They didn't stop to talk or even catch their breath. When Nick spotted a big outcropping of rocks higher up the mountain, they slogged up and sent a triumphant avalanche down the slope. The final downrush of stone buried the entrance. The two friends sat side by side, panting. At last, Nick looked at the mangled tripod and said, "I think Dad's gonna need a new one."

Then they both shook with relieved laughter.

Near evening, they found their way back to the first entrance to find their distraught parents, Angel, and a team of rangers frantically coordinating rescue operations. Even old Wesley Scoble had come to offer help.

But when Nick and Sarah tried to explain about the monster, the adults dismissed it as a run-in with an eagle that would have seemed more terrifying because of their being trapped underground. Only Angel and Wesley Scoble believed them. "There are dozens of caves on the dome. Could be anything—*lots* of anythings—hiding in them."

Then the shadow of a giant wing falling across the group of rescuers and rescued gave final, deadly proof of the youngsters' story.

Playland

It was almost Labor Day, and there were very few visitors coming to Playland in Beachcomber's Cove. But even at the height of summer, not many people had come to the amusement park. The crowds were all going five miles down the coast to the big, new, flashy Pacific Paradise Park. There folks could ride on loop-the-loop roller coasters, visit a haunted house full of laser-image ghosts and bogies, and try all kinds of state-of-the-art attractions.

Alec Grabinski felt sad that the new park made comfortable old Playland seem tired and dull to most people. To him, it remained a place of real excitement and magic. He had been coming to the Cove with his parents for nine of his eleven years. Every August the family rented a beachfront house for two weeks. He loved the town; he loved the amusement park. "I wish I could stay here forever," he told his mother one day.

"Be careful what you wish for," she said with a laugh. "You just might get your wish."

She said that as if it could be a bad thing, but he saw forever at the Cove as a wonderful, if impossible, dream.

On the Friday before the Sunday the family was to return home, Alec walked to the amusement park with his friend Brian Umeki. The Umekis had been coming to the Cove for three years. They lived in Fresno, and Alec's family lived in San Francisco, but the boys were pen pals when they weren't actually together.

"My dad says they're going to close Playland," said Brian. "People are all going down the road."

"But Playland has *always* been here," Alec said.

"Not anymore," said Brian. "They've already sold the land. They're gonna put up a lotta fancy houses."

"What about the rides and junk? What about Haunted Houseful?"

"I dunno. Tear it down? Maybe sell it to some other park? The Cove sure won't seem much fun without Playland."

Of all the things Playland had to offer, Haunted Houseful was Alec's favorite. He loved being scared, even if the ride had no laser ghosts or animatronic skeletons. He remembered his first ride in the jerky little cart that swiveled and rocked and turned unexpectedly. It had scared him wonderfully back then. It still did.

Of course, he knew all the twists and turns by heart—so he knew all the "surprises" that lay in wait for visitors. Cannibals stirring a stewpot that suddenly popped up an explorer in a pith helmet. Dracula (and his son, a minute later) rising from the grave. Skeletons dropping from the ceiling. A mummy lunging from a sarcophagus. Doors with painted flames ushering the cart into Satan's throne room, where the devil jabbed with a plastic pitchfork. And over everything, recorded screams and groans and roars and lunatic laughter.

His favorite was not so scary as it was weird. For a minute, as the car rattled along the track, it would swing to the left and move a few feet down a side track. A door would light up, painted to look like metal. Like a spaceship door, perhaps. In the middle was a round window like a porthole. For a minute, it would show a sky of unearthly blue. Then a face with burning red eyes would fill the porthole, then disappear—always too fast for Alec to see. No matter how many times he swore he was going to get a better look, the face came and went too fast. Then, with a hiss like escaping air, the painted metal door slid open, and he would be looking across a strange alien plain. There were graves closer in, and far away, at the foot of blue-gray mountains, was a city of towers and domes that sat mysterious and shadowy under two small moons, blue and silver.

Another hiss. The door closed. The car was jerked back into the darkness as the display dimmed to black.

This display affected him most when he was little. It still haunted him. Sometimes he imagined he would undo the safety bar that held him at the waist and go up to the door. He would get a close-up look at whatever was peeking through the porthole. Then he would step through into that graveyard plain and visit the city under the twin silver and blue moons.

But he didn't climb out. That would be silly, he reasoned. It would prove that the display was only cutouts and paint. And he wanted to believe it was so much more.

Since that first ride years before, the thrill of the place had never quite left him, for all his repeat visits. Usually there were others in the six-passenger car; sometimes, he had the ride thrillingly to himself. It didn't matter. He always felt there was a surprise or two waiting for him. Something so far unseen, around some corner yet unturned, through some unexpected doors, down some unlit stretch of track. Even Brian, his best friend and pen pal, looked at him like he was crazy when he tried to explain.

In fact, Brian admitted that he thought that the haunted house ride down the coast was better. He preferred the games in the arcade, letting Alec enjoy the Haunted Houseful alone.

But today Alec was determined to have his friend share what might be a last ride, if Playland was truly going to close.

The afternoon was foggy. The gray chill had kept all but a very few people from the amusement park. Most of them were in the games arcade, which was warmer because it was inside. This is where Brian wanted to head. Alec agreed to a trade-off: if he went to the arcade, Brian would ride through the Haunted Houseful with him. Brian found the ride boring. "Except for when

Dracula and his son rise from the grave all bloody. That's cool." He loved the fact that anyone who didn't know what to expect would be startled by the pop-up Dracula—then get a second jolt when his son popped up a minute later.

While Brian played Skee-Ball and Whack-a-Mole, Alec wandered around, trying the few games he hadn't tried before, feeling more and more sad that everything might be gone before the family returned the following August.

At the other entrance to the arcade was a glass booth with a mechanical witch inside. It was the "Wish Witch." She was draped in veils—more like a gypsy than a witch—sharp-featured, with staring red eyes of the same blood-red as her crimson lips. Only the upper half of a life-sized figure was visible through glass. The lower half of the booth was wood, hiding the machinery that ran the witch. The puppet looked silly—like a ticket seller at a movie theater. Almost no one spent four quarters to bring the Wish Witch to twitchy life. She had never interested Alec or Brian, because she offered no prizes—just wishes. And while he liked to think that some wishes could be granted, he doubted that the ugly old puppet in her glass-and-wood setting could help.

But he was out to try everything before Playland was gone. As he fed his quarters into the coin slot, he wondered if she'd even work. But as soon as his last quarter dropped, she came to herky-jerky life. "Make your wish," a tinny voice said through a square speaker-box beneath the place where glass met wood.

$1

"I wish Playland would never go away," Alec whispered at the silent figure. "I want to be able to enjoy Haunted Houseful again and again and again."

After a minute, the tinny voice said, "Let's see what the cards say."

The puppet hands moved back and forth, up and down, above the cards laid facedown on the ledge in front of the Wish Witch. The right hand dropped, touched a card, and lifted. The card, on a spring, flipped over. Alec couldn't see what it was.

"The seven of spades," the tinny voice announced. "Your wish is granted."

The card flipped back to facedown. The Wish Witch relaxed into stillness.

"What a rip-off," said Brian. Alec hadn't heard him approach, so he jumped. "You scared already?" teased Brian. "What do you need the Haunted Houseful ride for?"

"You promised," said Alec, getting some of his cool back.

There was no one in line at the Haunted Houseful. The owner's nephew, Tony, who worked summers, sold them their tickets. He helped them into a cart—each got his own two-passenger seat, Alec in front and Brian behind him. Tony fastened the safety bars across their waists. "You're my last riders," he said, waving to Consuela who ran the Tilt-a-Whirl down the boardwalk. "I got things I gotta do."

The cart lurched forward, through the swinging doors with the hand-lettered banner warning, "Abandon hope all ye who enter."

Brian's sighs and fidgets under the lock-bar made clear to Alec how dumb his friend thought the ride was. He only paid attention to the bloody Dracula and son display.

Once again, Alec experienced everything as fresh and new. He didn't want it to end. He thought how great it would be if the puppet witch had truly granted his wish.

Then they burst through the swinging doors that separated the haunted dark from the sunlight. The cart rolled to the loading platform, slowed. There was no Tony to lift the safety bars as they glided to a halt. He was probably hanging out with Consuela, Alec thought. He tried the bar, but it was locked in place, keeping him a prisoner. Then the cart lurched forward and began to pick up speed. "Hey!" yelled Brian. "No more."

But the bars across their waists held the boys fast. They lurched into the dark again; this time the ride seemed to speed up.

"I think my safety bar is broken," said Alec, pushing up on it with the palms of his hands. "Help," shouted Brian, struggling with his own restraint. "Hang on!" Alec warned his friend, as the car spun right, spun left, spun in a circle. The cannibals' dinner popped up. Skeletons dropped. Dracula and son rose from their shared grave. The car only slowed for the hissing metal door to open and show the far city below the mountains and twin moons. To Alec, this part of the ride seemed to go in slow motion. Then they were back tearing full speed ahead. The spinning and jerking was beginning to hurt his neck and give him a headache. Brian was whimpering behind him, slapping at the bar in frustration.

The cart slammed through the exit doors.

Sunlight dazzled Alec's eyes. It took him a minute to blink away the blur and realize that Tony had not returned.

The cars slowed teasingly as they neared the landing platform. "Help!" the boys yelled. But no one heard. Tony was still gone. "This ride has gone crazy!"

The car shot forward.

"Abandon hope . . ." and they were inside. Right. Left. Right. Left. Around. Dracula popped up. His son followed.

"I got it," yelled Brian, managing to raise the bar off his waist. "Let me help you."

"Don't stand up!" cried Alec.

But his warning came too late. The car spun suddenly. He heard Brian scream as the boy was launched into the darkness. A minute later there was a *thump!* and Brian's cry was cut off.

Alec screamed himself as the car took him right, left, around. He had a pause for the mysterious city under the blue and silver moons, then he was slammed left, slammed right, and smashed through the exit doors. No slowing now. The bar stayed locked in place, no matter how hard he pushed on it. "Abandon . . ."—then it was herky-jerky through the dark. Cannibals, skeletons, Dracula and son all shooting past in a blur—only this time the rising plaster vampire display revealed Brian's head and shoulders. He had apparently been slammed into the figures and caught in the mechanism. His eyes, open but not seeing, still had a look of stunned surprise.

"Be careful what you wish for," Alec's mother had said.

He felt sick at heart for his friend, who had been caught on the edge of his wish. In a moment Brian had become part of his favorite scare. As the car rocketed on through the dark, Alec suddenly felt sure he knew where he was headed.

His head seemed to be whirling faster than the cart. Lights, dark, bright, dark, the cart was moving incredibly fast.

There was a final, unthinkably violent jerk. He felt a sharp pain as his head snapped forward and backward. There was a single crunch that seemed to be inside and outside his head at the same time. Then he lost consciousness for a minute.

Then he was in a cart moving slowly ahead. There was a silence as if his ears were plugged up, like what had happened to him once when the jet he was traveling on landed. Everything was happening in slow motion.

He was heading straight for the door that opened on the graveyard and the curious city beyond. The red-painted eyes studied him through the porthole; now he recognized them as belonging to the Wish Witch. The door hissed open. The cart continued to glide forward, beyond the point where it would have turned aside in the real world. Beyond the point where the door would have closed on the brief glimpse of graveyard and towering city.

Somewhere, Alec was certain, a cart was continuing to rocket and rock through light and dark, carrying the form of a boy whose head tossed limply from side to side on a neck like a broken flower stalk.

But that was someplace that no longer mattered here (wherever *here* was).

Behind him, the mysterious metal door hissed shut, and the cart rolled on past silent graves toward the shadowy city on the edge of forever.

smoke

Katie was surprised at how the smell of burning lingered in her senses so long after the fire. In her dreams, the air around the gutted shell of their house was thick with the odor of water-soaked ash, even though it had been weeks since the fire. The shade trees nearest the house were twisted black shapes in the evening; many trees that stood some distance away had charred branches or crisped leaves, and were clearly dying.

The smoky odor followed her everywhere, though it was worst here, in her dreams, where the fire had taken her parents from her. Here the smell of the smoke woke her choking in the night, where smoky billows blinded her and swallowed her cries of "Mommy! Daddy! Where are you?" From deep within the smoky madness, she heard them crying her name.

All she could think about was that her last words to her mommy and daddy had been "I hate you both," because they had not let her spend the night at a sleep-over with her friends. But she really didn't hate them—had never meant the words. Somehow, she had to take the words back and assure them of her love.

Through the smoke-filled nightmare she had plunged, arms stretched out, groping for her parents, who were screaming her name somewhere just out of reach. Then she encountered the flames behind the smoke; she was driven back by the heat that set her pajama sleeves on fire. The teddy bears and dolls on the shelf above her bed were suddenly wrapped in blazing fur and blazing dresses. In terror, she had run back into the smoke, had run from the frantic shouts and screams, had run on and on into the smoky blackness that swallowed her up. Looking for her parents, wanting to hug them and pull them to safety after the hateful, hurtful things she had said. From a distance she heard fire engines and guessed that the Robinsons, who lived down the road, had seen the flames and had called the town's volunteer fire department.

More smoke—deeper, thicker, choking—and she could no longer hear her parents. Voices were shouting, more sirens, and then a cry of, "Here's one!"

She couldn't remember anything more until she woke in a bed in Grandma's house, the house she hadn't been in since she was seven, more than two years ago. She felt confused. She couldn't remember the last time she had seen Grandma. It was in a hospital—but then she hadn't been the one lying down; her grandmother had been. It was all very confusing. But she loved the old woman. She remembered she had kissed her the last time she saw her. *Before the fire.* Everything was "before the fire" or "now" to Katie.

Grandma patted her arm and said, "She's awake." Katie saw someone else in the room. She recognized the tall man from the pictures she had seen in Grandma's house, though she had never met her grandfather before. The man had gone away long before Katie was born. Now he was back.

Everything was wrong somehow. She couldn't remember lots of things.

"Why is Grandpa back?" the girl asked.

"You need the two of us," said Grandma, as if that explained it all.

She slept again. But dreaming of the fire woke Katie up. She tried to sit up suddenly, calling for her parents, until Grandma pushed her gently back into the pillows mounded behind her head. Now she felt too weak to struggle.

"There was a fire," she said. "Where are Mommy and Daddy?"

"Oh, Baby Girl," said Grandma, leaning over to hug her. "They're gone far away. But, in time, with God's mercy, we'll all be together again."

"You can count on it, Mavourneen," said Grandpa.

"That's a funny word," said Katie sleepily.

"It's an Irish word," he explained. "It means 'My darling.' You'll always be 'Katie Mavourneen' to your grandma and me."

Grandma was as loving as ever. Grandpa tried to keep her entertained with stories of his own childhood in Ireland, and tales of leprechauns and giants and heroes like Finn McCool. He taught Katie how to play cribbage. But the girl only grew more restless. Her grandparents' house felt strange. It was just as she remembered it from visits—down a tree-shaded road far outside of town. Of course, it had only been Grandma's house, since Grandpa had gone away long ago. But, though she recognized the house she had played in so often as a younger child, it seemed *odd* to her in some ways. The wall of trees looked thicker, their leafy canopy keeping out any view of the sun or moon and stars, so that light and darkness seemed to sift down through the branches like flour when Grandma was baking. There seemed to be plenty of food in the house, though neither of the adults went shopping, and no delivery person brought groceries. In fact, in all the time she had been there, no one had come to call.

The telephone was broken; the little black-and-white TV got only one station that ran old movies and comedy series over and over; the radio produced only static. Grandpa played old records that sounded scratchy and tinny, with singers like Enrico Caruso and John McCormack—people Katie had never heard of, singing songs that were old-fashioned or in foreign languages and nothing she wanted to hear. She decided it was like living in some strange place where time had gone backward to the way her grandparents remembered things.

And the memory-smell of smoke filled the little house, though only she was aware of it. It clung to the curtains and rose up from the carpets with every step she took. The air had a faint blue haze that often stung her eyes to tears, though her grandparents never noticed anything amiss. For the child the smoke was as persistent as the memory of her father's frantic shouts and her mother's screams, "Katie! Katie!" Every night she dreamed they were standing on the steps of the burned house calling to her, "Come home, Katie. Katie, come back to us."

I want to go look for my mommy and daddy," she said one evening as Grandpa pulled out the cribbage board and little wooden pegs for keeping score, and Grandma settled in for another night of knitting that she worked on forever without completing a sweater or scarf or anything.

Katie's grandpa glanced across the dining room table at Grandma; they shared a worried look. Then Grandpa said gently, "They're in another world, Mavourneen."

"Then they'd be ghosts. Ghosts come back. I believe it," she said stubbornly. Then she quickly added, "I just want to see them one more time."

"You'll see them in God's own time, " Grandma said as she began counting loops along her knitting needle.

"Now!"

"*Musha!* It's not fitting, a meeting of the living and the dead," Grandpa said.

"Then you do believe in ghosts?" Katie persisted.

Grandpa sighed and looked at the cribbage board. "Yes, them poor earthbound spirits. They can't move on because something holds them back."

"Mommy and Daddy need to see me as much as I want to see them," the girl insisted. "Every night they come to me in a dream. They want me to go back to our old house."

"It's nothing but a wreck, Mavourneen. There's been no fixing up since the night of the fire. You're here, and your folks are gone away. Let things be as they are."

"But they come back to our house, looking for me." An idea came to her. "Maybe, if I could just see them, they could rest easier. I know I'd feel better."

"Such things are not in God's plan," said Grandma, with a sharp little nod of her head, as if that settled the matter.

Grandfather pointed hopefully at the cribbage board.

"I don't want to play," the girl said. "I just want to go to bed."

The dream came again: her parents, standing in front of the burned-out house, calling to her. Katie awoke nearly choking from the smell and taste of smoke. She was surer than ever that her parents were not at rest in the waking world any more than they were at peace in her dreams. The certainty was growing in her that she could find them again. She was sure the three of them could somehow manage to reach across the border between the living and the dead. They would hug, and she would promise them that she had always loved them and would continue to love them till they all met again in what her grandparents called, "the Blessed Place."

But every time she proposed going to what was left of her home to find her parents, Katie's guardians refused.

"In time, earthbound spirits move on," said Grandpa. "To mix the living and the dead makes things more worrisome. That's why it's not allowed."

"How do *you* know?" Katie argued.

"We know what we know," said Grandma. Her tone of voice said, *That's an end to it.*

But the haunting smell of smoke grew stronger. At times when Katie was wide awake, she thought she could hear her parents calling her from a great distance. To the girl, this was proof that her parents had not surrendered to the call of the Blessed Place. But she had to find them. For whatever reason, they couldn't come to her.

Two nights later, her mind made up, Katie slipped out of the house when she was certain her grandparents were fast asleep. She left a note to assure them she was all right and would return when she had done what she had to do. She was sure they would guess where she had gone. But what could they do? The phone was still dead. Neither one of her grandparents could drive. Katie couldn't remember how she had gotten to their house in the first place. Had an ambulance or neighbor driven her? It was one of the many bits of memory lost to her since the night of the fire. But there was no way her grandparents could come after her, unless they walked to the nearest neighbor's house—a good half-mile away. Surely Katie would have more than enough time to take care of her unfinished business with her parents.

The world—with moonlight softened and scattered by the masses of cloud overhead—seemed strange to Katie. The moon-silvered trees seemed as towering and twisted as trees in a dream. She ignored the strangeness, thinking only of her parents, their ghostly shapes—faint as smoke-haze, voices whisper-soft—reaching out to her. What would it be like to hug a ghost? she wondered. Like holding empty air? It didn't matter. The hugging was all that mattered.

Katie hurried down the gravel road from the darkened cottage. She wished she had her bike, but it was back at the house, in the garage that had probably burned with the house. She imagined her Super-Speed-8 shrunk to a clump of melted metal and matted rubber. She pushed the unhappy thought aside.

She ran on. The gravel crunched under her Nikes. The trees were a blur of silvery trunks and branches, with inky spaces between and under them. She felt as if she were running through a dream, but she ran on. All she could think of was her parents waiting on the steps of the house that was no longer there.

Faster! she urged herself. She fell into the rhythm that had made her the star of the girls track team at school, back when such things mattered. All that mattered now was Mommy and Daddy and *home*.

When she reached the road leading to town, she was surprised that there were no cars anywhere. And the cloud-covered sky still hid the moon and stars. As she ran along the shoulder of the road, she had the momentary feeling that she was in a world empty of anyone but herself and her grandparents, who were still asleep. The damp air held a smoky smell. And the thickness of it swallowed up the sound of her pounding feet.

With every step nearer home, the smell of smoke grew stronger. The world around her was a blur. There was nothing but the smell of smoke, the road, and her need to reach home.

Katie lost track of time. She didn't realize how far she had come so quickly, but she had reached the gaudy tile gateposts her father had put up to be sure no guests missed the turnoff to their house. In the strange night glow, the tiles looked only like different shades of silver-gray—not the rainbow colors they were in sunlight. Down the road, where the town was, the girl saw only a shadowy mass of buildings and trees piled against the skies. There were no lights. The power must have failed, Katie decided. Perhaps it was part of the same problem that had left the phones dead and reduced the TV to one station.

Nothing mattered, however, except that she was almost home. Now the air was dense with silver-blue smoke, as if the house were burning again. She still couldn't hear the slap of her shoes on the asphalt. The smoke was thicker than ever. It swallowed up sound.

Then, suddenly, she burst through the smoke as though she were running through a wall. The smell clung to her jeans and jacket and hair and hands, but it was behind her and tangled in the trees around the wreck of the house. There was a circle of clear air around the house, so she could see the moon and stars, though it was like looking into the sky from the bottom of a well whose walls were made of smoke.

The oak tree in the front yard had its leaves burned away, and its crisped branches clutched like skeletal hands at the sky and the house it once shaded. That house was all but gone. The roof had fallen in; the windows had been blown out by the heat, leaving bits of glass sparkling like stars in the blackened grass. Her mother's roses were twisted sticks showing here and there a charred blossom or leaf. The smell of smoke was faint, but clung to everything. She started up the heat-cracked path, seeing the marks of big tires—probably from the fire engines, on the cement. Though the front of the house was crisscrossed with yellow plastic ribbons warning "Danger—Do Not Cross," she ignored them and climbed the short flight of concrete steps to stand on the buckled porch. She tried the knob on the front door. The handle turned but the door, its paint bubbled and scorched, wouldn't open at first. But when she pushed on it, she was able to shove it back far enough to enter.

"Mommy? Daddy?" she called into the darkness inside. Then she listened. There was no answer. She went

into what was left of the entranceway. The living room to her left was a jumble of ruined furniture and rugs and drapes, lit by a little moonlight that crept past the plywood sheets blocking the windows. The stairway and back of the house were nothing but wreckage. Tumbled ceramic roof tiles mixed with boards and broken bits of furniture—the remains of the upstairs bedrooms. Her room. Her parents' room. Everything gone.

"Mommy! Daddy!" she called more loudly.

A beam and part of the destroyed roof shifted. There was a sound like a sigh. The house breathed out a choking billow of smoke—thick and damp—that clung to her skin and eyes, caught in her nose and throat. Coughing, Katie retreated into the clear air outside, rubbing her smoke-filmed eyes.

They were waiting for her at the bottom of the front steps. At first they seemed blurry and faint, as though they were made of smoke. They were rubbing their eyes—filled with tears and wonder—as if they couldn't see her any more clearly than she could see them. Then everything swam into focus. She saw that it really was them. They seemed to see her clearly at the same instant.

For what seemed like an eternity, no one spoke. Then Katie cried, "You came!"

Her mother stretched one hand out to her daughter, and put her other hand to her mouth to stifle a sob. Katie's father just said, "Honey," in a raspy voice as though his throat was dry or damaged.

Then Katie bounded down the steps, bursting a strand of yellow warning tape like a racer crossing the finish line. She hurled herself into their arms. And they felt as warm and real as the love that had brought them all together across unimaginable distances. She felt so happy, she wished her grandparents could be here to share this joy. How wrong they had been to try and stop her from coming!

"I've missed you so much," she cried, her head swiveling back and forth between the two loved faces. "There was fire and smoke everywhere, and then you were gone. And all I could think was that the last thing I said to you was 'I hate you.' And I *don't*. I *never* could. I love you both so much!"

"We know. We always knew."

"That's what Grandma and Grandpa Riordan say."

"You've seen them?" her mother asked, as if this was surprising.

"Sure. They've been taking care of me since the fire. But they didn't want me to look for you."

"Why?" asked her father.

"They said it's not a good idea for living people and—well, *others*—" she couldn't bring herself to say *ghosts*— "to meet. Everybody's supposed to wait and meet in what they call the Blessed Place. But I heard you calling me in my dreams every night. I had to see you and tell you how much I've always loved you." She had an arm around each of her parents now. She never would let them go. And they clung to her as if they felt the same.

"You've been in our thoughts every minute of every day," said her mother.

"What's it like where you are?" Katie asked.

"We're over in town," Daddy said, "Staying with friends—the Johnsons."

"Then it's just like here?" Katie wondered. "How did the Johnsons die? Was it a car crash?"

Her mother looked confused. Then she said, "All that matters is that we've found you. It means so much to know you're being taken care of by my ma and pa, and that we'll all be together some day."

They hugged fiercely once again. Now Katie noticed that the smell of smoke was turning to the smell of burned roses and then to the sweet remembered smell of her mother's rose garden on a warm spring afternoon.

"Can't we stay together forever?" Katie begged.

"It's not the way things work, Mavourneen," said her grandpa, gently placing his hand on Katie's right shoulder. "The living have to get on with their lives."

"And the dead with their deaths," said Grandma, placing her hand on Katie's other shoulder.

"How did you get here? I didn't hear a car! I didn't hear anything!" the puzzled girl exclaimed.

Her mother and father had taken a step back from the others.

"Ma! Pa!" her mother said, so softly she could barely hear her. "You really are here."

"Sure, an' you don't think we'd leave our Mavourneen to find her way alone," said Grandpa.

"But we must go now," said Grandma. "And there won't be any more meetings until the Lord's good time."

A memory came to Katie. She remembered the last time she had seen her Grandma. It had been at the woman's funeral, kissing her goodbye. And Grandpa, she now recalled, had died before she was born.

Now she understood so much that she hadn't understood since the fire.

Katie's grandparents lifted their hands from her shoulders. She hugged her parents one more time. But now they felt like little more in her arms than a puff of smoke.

"Take good care of her!" Katie's mother said. Her father called out something else. Katie saw his lips moving, but she could no longer hear his words.

"We'll go now," said Grandma.

"Back to your house?" Katie asked.

"We'll be goin' on a bit farther, Mavourneen," Grandpa said.

"To the Blessed Place?"

"Indeed," said Grandma with her decisive nod.

Then the silver night was gone. The burned house was gone. The blackened trees and tire-scored road were gone. The smell of smoke was gone, replaced with the smell of roses everywhere, and a comforting light like a thousand sunrises embraced Katie and her two loving guardians.

In front of the burned-out shell of what had been the family's house, Katie's parents peered into the now-empty air, held each other's hands in tenderness and joy, and walked slowly back to their parked car, leaning their heads against each other.

Mrs. Moonlight (Señora Claro de Luna)

You are a bad girl, Maria Luisa!" her *abuela* scolded.

The nine-year-old shrugged. She hadn't meant to break Grandmother Amalia's vase. It had happened because she was chasing Dulzura, the old woman's cat. It was the cat's fault for refusing to be caught and petted and perhaps dressed in a doll's skirt and gloves—for making the girl run though the house after her. When the cat had skittered under the table behind the couch, the girl had followed and snared the cat by one hind leg, only to have the cat turn and scratch her hand. Startled, the girl had jerked back, knocking the table, with fatal results for the vase.

"Blame Dulzura," she protested. She held up her hand to show four red lines, with a tiny bead of blood on one, where the cat had raked her. She began to cry, "See how she hurt me. Wicked *gata!*"

Amalia Lopez made a face. Much as she loved her granddaughter, her patience was wearing thin. The child ignored the simplest rules of good behavior, did as she pleased, then argued or lied or wept every time she was caught doing wrong. And this was happening more and more often.

"The cat isn't wicked," Amalia said. "It is someone else."

Maria Luisa burst into tears. "You hate me! You love that cat more than you love your own granddaughter. I want my *mamá*. I don't want to stay here anymore." Her shoulders shook as she sobbed and sobbed.

Her grandmother—in a sudden panic at the child's weeping—forgot her anger and her resolve. She pulled the child to her. Her daughter—Maria Luisa's mother—had left the girl in her keeping in Santa Rosita, New Mexico, while she went on business to Dallas, Texas. Amalia knew that her daughter spoiled the girl terribly: she had proof of it every day. But she also knew her daughter wanted to give Maria Luisa the best life possible, since the girl's father had abandoned them just after the child was born.

Amalia had offered her daughter and grandchild shelter. She hadn't realized that she was going to become a second mother to the girl, as her daughter's ever-more-important work took her on longer and longer trips throughout the Southwest.

Amalia was happy enough to take care of the girl, whom she loved deeply. If only the child would love her back! Or respect her, at least! But Maria Luisa was an increasingly willful child—not only with her *abuela*, but also with her *mamá*. Her grandmother gave every ounce of love she could to the child—wrung her heart out—but the child just drank her love dry, then found new ways to twist her heart.

They sat for a long time, while Amalia soothed the child, then tenderly dressed the scratches and assured her that Dulzura didn't hate her but was only defending herself because Maria Luisa had frightened her.

"*Gata loca*," the girl said sourly. "That cat is crazy."

"Just be gentle," her grandmother insisted, still rocking the child on her lap, though the girl's tears had long since dried up—if they were real tears at all, she sighed to herself.

"*Sí, sí, sí*," said the child impatiently, squirming out of her grandmother's embrace. She grabbed a striped ball from beside the door, then ran out onto the patio to play.

Amalia just shook her head, and crooked her finger at Dulzura, who poked her head out from under the couch. After a quick side-to-side glance to be sure Maria Luisa was nowhere around, the cat came and curled up in the old woman's lap.

"*Ay!* What are we to do about that child?" asked Amalia.

But the cat, safe and comfortable, just purred contentedly. Soon the two were fast asleep.

Outside, Maria Luisa soon grew tired of bouncing the ball off the house (forbidden by her grandmother) and the garden walls. She was sure the hurt done to her *abuela's* roses and other plants would not be discovered until her mother was home, and then scolding meant nothing.

She gave the ball a final kick, sending it over the shoulder-high adobe wall into the sandy waste beyond. *Now what?* she wondered, not interested in searching for the ball. Her mother would always buy her a new one. Then she saw a line of ants, at the edge of the patio. They were going and coming through a crack in the wall in two lines to their nest under a clump of dried grass. As she bent to look closer, her fingers splayed out on the patio, and several ants scrabbled over her fingers.

"Ah!" she cried in disgust, standing up and brushing them off. "I'll show you!"

But how? Then she remembered the magnifying glass her grandmother used to read the small print on medicine bottles or in letters from friends who wrote as though they were in a contest to see who could squeeze the most words onto a single page.

She glanced in through the patio door. Her *abuela* was asleep, with Dulzura curled on her lap.

She promised herself she'd get revenge on the scratching cat soon enough. But the ants held her interest at the moment. Sliding the door open as quietly as possible, she went to her grandmother's desk, took out the big, round magnifying glass, and hurried back to the patio's edge. There she used the glass to focus the sun's rays on individual ants, tormenting the panicky workers, burning several to ashes. Growing impatient, she kept the hot point of sunlight on the cluster of dried grass sheltering the entrance to the anthill. To her satisfaction, the dry grass quickly burst into flame, which leapt from the first to a second and then a third clump of grass.

Maria Luisa scuttled back from the flames. As she did, the magnifying glass dropped onto the patio and shattered. Now five or six clumps of grass were burning.

"What have you done?" shouted Amalia, who had been wakened by the restive cat, made nervous by the fire and smell of something burning.

"It wasn't my fault!" Maria Luisa whined.

Amalia ignored her and grabbed the garden hose. In a few minutes she had doused the blazing clumps of grass, but she continued to soak them in case any spark remained.

"*Niña!* You could have burned the house down!" cried her grandmother.

"I don't know how it happened," the girl said sulkily.

"And I suppose this wasn't your fault either," said Amalia, using the toe of her shoe to push the broken magnifying glass toward her granddaughter.

"Dulzura broke it," said the girl.

"What an amazing cat I have!" said Amalia. "While she is asleep on my lap, she takes my magnifying glass from the desk and sets fire to the garden. Extraordinary!"

"You don't believe me! You *never* believe me!" wailed Maria Luisa.

"Enough of your tears—real or pretend," said Amalia sternly. "I must warn you that so much bad behavior has put you in danger of *Señora Claro de Luna*. Mrs. Moonlight comes at night to catch wicked children who mix the light of truth with the darkness of lies. She comes in the moonlight, to take troublemakers away to the moon. There they must clean her house and tend her garden and polish her silver until the end of time."

"You're making that up," the girl said. "It's an old story you're using to scare me. I'll tell my *mamá* you were scaring me."

"Some stories are old because they have truth in them, and must be told over and over."

Maria Luisa stuck out her tongue. "You're a mean, lying *abeula*, and I hate you, and I don't want to stay here, and I want my mother now, or I'll scream and scream until she comes for me." And she did scream herself hoarse, until the desperate old woman called her daughter in Dallas and told her she'd have to come home early, that things had grown impossible with the child.

Wearily, her daughter said yes, she would return, her business was really done. She could afford to come home early. "Put Maria Luisa on the phone," she said at last.

With a smile of victory, the girl took the phone. "*Abuela* is always mad at me for no reason. And her cat scratched me. And she's trying to scare me with stupid old ghost stories that I don't believe." In no time, the girl worked herself up to tears again. From across the room, her grandmother, stroking the cat, shook her head as soothing words of love poured from the phone into her granddaughter's ear.

When she had hung up the phone, Maria Luisa turned and said, "You can't be mean to me anymore. *Mamá* says so."

"So my wishes count for nothing in my own house?" her grandmother replied. "But I want peace under my roof. So I will only say that I try to love you; Dulzura would be kind to you if you were kind to her; and Mrs. Moonlight is real. So have a care, child."

But the girl just turned away and flounced out onto the patio, not bothering to close the sliding glass door or the screen door. The old woman sighed and shut them both. Through the glass she saw the girl looking at the burned grass with a smile that indicated she was proud of what she had done. Amalia decided she would have to talk to her daughter: something had to be done about the child who was growing more wicked every day. But in her heart she knew such talk would be useless. The girl twisted her mother around her finger as easily as a bean vine twists around a garden stake.

That night Maria Luisa awoke suddenly. It was very late. Her bedside clock with the glow-in-the-dark face showed her it was 1:13 a.m. The house was asleep; her *abuela* would be dreaming in her bed, with Dulzura curled at her feet.

The full desert moon was shining brightly over a low range of hills. Scattered silver clouds looked like wings. The night seemed bright as day. The girl was hungry. She had refused to eat much of her dinner to get back at her grandmother for so much scolding. In return, her grandmother had denied her any of the honey-sweetened cake that should have been her dessert. The cake had gone back into the kitchen cupboard, untouched by either of them. She would help herself to the cake, and deal with the older woman's anger in the morning.

Quietly, she pushed back the light blanket and slid out of bed. But as she stood in the doorway of the living room where moonlight flooded in through the tall windows, Maria Luisa thought of her grandmother's story of Mrs. Moonlight and paused, still in shadow. Then she laughed at her fear, and said, "*Abuela's loca*—just like her cat."

She started for the kitchen, but froze when a sudden hiss came from the brightest pool of moonlight. Just the sort of hiss a rattlesnake made. Had one of the deadly creatures slipped into the house? Maybe one time when she had left a door open just to annoy her grandmother?

Only daring to turn her head, because a rattler would be attracted by a sudden movement, she looked more closely at the puddle of light. There was no snake. She sighed so loudly in relief she was afraid she might wake her grandmother.

But there was something odd about the moon pool. A swirl of dust motes was gathering above it—wisps of sparkling silver flecks. As she watched, hypnotized, they thickened into a silvery mist. Now the mist was swirling like a dust devil, growing more solid, taller. It began to take on the shape of a tall woman in long, pale skirts. Her face was so veiled in white lace that Maria Luisa couldn't see her eyes, but she was sure they were staring at her. The woman had long, fingerless white gloves. Her bony fingers ended in nails like talons that shone silver. She had many silver bracelets on her arms and a silver ring on each finger.

She pointed at Maria Luisa, then crooked her long finger. "Come, naughty child," she said.

But the terrified girl shrank back into the triangle of shadow in the corner between two of the windows. She tried to call, *"Abuela!"* but the word caught in her throat, which was as dry as the bottom of an arroyo. The sound reached no further than the ghostly woman, who gave a hiss as she peered into the girl's hiding place.

The bent finger coaxed again. "I can't see you in the shadows," she said, her voice as sweet now as Grandma's honey cake. "Come out into the light." Maria Luisa only scrunched herself into a ball as deep in the shadows as possible. She pressed her hands to her mouth, so her frightened breathing wouldn't give her hiding place away.

A sharp hiss. Then the veiled figure took a step closer. The silver claws pressed against the shadows as if the darkness were a pane of thick, tinted glass she couldn't reach through. The ghastly veiled head came close, bobbing with snake-like darts all around, as if looking for, but unable to see, the girl. Maria Luisa was chewing on her knuckles to keep from screaming. Why didn't her grandmother wake up? Why wasn't her mother here to save her? They didn't love her enough, she thought angrily. She didn't dare to try calling out for her grandmother. Surely the creature there would hear and find her in the dark.

The ghostly hands, like big pale spiders, crawled over the shadow as if seeking a weak spot, a point where Mrs. Moonlight (for Maria Luisa had guessed right away who

this was) could reach through and grab her and carry her off to the moon.

She has no power in the shadows, the girl kept reminding herself. *I will be safe if I stay in the dark until morning.*

"You must come with me, *niña.*" The voice sounded kind, but Maria Luisa could hear a note of growing anger underneath the honey. Suddenly the figure balled one hand into a fist and slammed it against the shadowed wall. The *thump* made the girl jump.

"Reach out your hand to me, *niña,*" the figure insisted. "If you make me wait for the shadows to go and my lovely light to fill the corner, things are going to be much worse for you."

For a moment, the girl thought she could see silver teeth glittering under the veils. Burning eyes round and shiny as two silver dollars seemed to lock on her own. The hunger in those eyes forced a little sound of fright out of her.

With a hiss, the veiled face flattened against the shadow. "Oh, I see you, I see you now. The moon is shifting. The shadows are growing smaller." There was no hint of sweetness now. Only rage. "Naughty child to disobey, but you won't escape me much longer."

It was true. The changing position of the moon was shrinking her shadowed hiding place. Maria Luisa pressed herself as far back into the corner as she could.

The moonlight continued to edge toward her feet. The veiled figure stood still and silent now. Waiting—like Dulzura when she was hunting a bird or lizard. Waiting to pounce, eyes like pools of mercury fixed on the shadow hiding the girl, claws ready.

The moon continued on its path across the heavens. Light drank the shadows. The moonlight edged closer to her slippers. She tried again to call for her grandmother, but fear continued to rob her of her voice.

Still the moonlight advanced. Now the shadow barrier was no thicker than sheer silk. The silver nails of one bony hand slashed at it, but still couldn't get through. Still it was only a matter of moments before her safety was gone.

Tears filled Maria Luisa's eyes. She wanted to blame her mother and grandmother and Mrs. Moonlight for her misery, but she realized she had brought this on herself. Broken vases and magnifying glasses, a frightened cat and tormented ants, and a loving mother and grandmother endlessly troubled and bullied by her lies and tears—thoughts of all these things rose to accuse her. In despair, she admitted she had brought the moonlit horror upon herself.

She whimpered. Mrs. Moonlight quivered with excitement at the sound.

Closer came the moonlight.

Closer came the veiled figure.

Closer—

The girl was standing up now, arms at her sides, hiding in the last corner of shadow.

The claws were following the retreating edge of the shadow, ready to grab the girl in a deadly embrace. In a moment the shifting moon would put her at the mercy of the veiled horror.

"Abuela!" Maria Luisa screamed, finding her voice at last.

"Too late!" cried Mrs. Moonlight, with a series of sharp hisses that the girl guessed was a kind of terrible laughter.

Moonlight touched her shoulders; the silver-tipped claws dug into the material of her nightdress.

Then the overhead light snapped on. Mrs. Moonlight vanished in the brightness that banished moonlight and shadows together.

"Now what are you up to?" asked Grandmother, her hand still on the light switch. But her anger turned to concern when she saw how pale her grandchild was, as she watched the girl slip to her knees on the floor in the corner of the room. She ran and gathered the child into her arms.

"She was here!" the girl sobbed. "Mrs. Moonlight."

"Nonsense," said the old woman. "She's only a story. You had a dream. You must have been walking in your sleep. Oh, I wish I had never told you about *Señora Claro de Luna!"*

"But she's real," Maria Luisa protested. "When you put on the light, you scared her away." She buried her face in the old woman's shoulder. "I'm sorry for what I did. I'll be good. Really I will. I don't want Mrs. Moonlight to get me."

"Poor child! Poor child! There's no such thing," the woman insisted. "You dreamed it, *niña*. I'll show you—"

And before her granddaughter could stop her, Amalia snapped off the lights. "You see, there's only the pretty moonlight. Nothing to be afraid of. Forget my foolish story."

With a triumphant *hiss-hiss-hiss* of laughter, Mrs. Moonlight flew through the window, grabbed Maria Luisa by the hair, and sped away with her. To Amalia's horror, the moonlit figures passed through the closed window as if they had no more substance than moonbeams. By the time she reached the window herself, Amalia saw nothing more than entwined pale smudges racing along the last rays toward the setting moon.

Hungry Ghosts

The family picnic was still going on, but thirteen-year-old Michael Choy had grown bored with the games his little brother and sisters and all his noisy cousins wanted to play. The ferry ride to Angel Island from San Francisco had been fun, and lunch had been good and filling: a mix of old-style foods like pork buns and sesame balls, as well as the hot dogs and hamburgers the younger people insisted on. He had even humored his grandmother and mother and aunts when they had put a tray of food to one side for the hungry family ghosts. The women were always setting aside an offering for the ghosts in the belief that this would encourage the spirits to bring them good fortune and luck. Michael liked the yearly Hungry Ghost Festival—though he didn't believe in ancestor ghosts any more than he believed in the ghosts and witches of Halloween. But many adults believed. They would warn the children of the family, "Don't go out alone at night, or a wandering ghost might possess you." Still, however silly the stories were, Michael felt they made the day even creepier.

But in the warm afternoon, the ghosts' meal was only drawing flies. The afternoon was really a drag, and there were still several hours before they would board the ferry for the return to San Francisco. The adults sat around and talked. The other kids played kickball or other games that were uninteresting to Michael, or they flew kites.

"Having fun?" asked Uncle Andrew, who had left his older brother—Michael's father—and several other male relatives discussing business and real estate. The still-young man was Michael's favorite uncle—someone who was much more interested in talking sports or action movies or pop music.

"Not really," said Michael, shrugging.

"I tried to get the others interested in hiking around the island. But no one seems to care. I'm going to go. It's been almost two years since I was last here. There's a lot to see. Want to come? I promise we'll be back in time for the last ferry out."

"Sure!"

The two set off across the grassy picnic grounds around the cove where the ferries docked. They walked uphill to the trail that ran all the way around the island's edge. Andrew, who had been a history major in college, and who volunteered at the Chinese Historical Society in

San Francisco, told his nephew lots of interesting facts as they wandered along. They wandered down a short side trail to look at the old buildings of the West Garrison.

"This was the first military base on the island," said Andrew. "It was built around the time of the Civil War and was kept up by the army until after the Second World War." Michael found himself imagining what it must have been like being a soldier in this lonely space more than a hundred years ago. Did ghosts still linger, drilling under the moon when the island's visitors had gone home? And did they have any family left to bring them offerings of food? The boy gave himself a pleasant little shiver imagining the ghosts marching endlessly in moonlight, growing thinner and hungrier. What would happen if someone visited the place late at night? he wondered. The start of a great scary movie, he answered himself.

Another side trip took them down to the beach, where Andrew sat watching the waves while Michael went beachcombing, finding interesting, sea-polished bits of colored glass and wave-sculpted bits of metal. He put these in his pocket as his uncle climbed to his feet, brushed sand off the seat of his pants, and said, "Ready to go? There's plenty more to see."

The paved trail turned to dirt. Two young women, marching along with the stride of serious hikers, called brisk "hellos" as they passed and were quickly lost around a curve. The day was getting hotter. Michael and Andrew paused to sip some of their bottled water. They passed an old missile site, the entrance to a Coast Guard station, and paused several times to look across the bay to San Francisco. The road was paved again, and rising slightly. Down the hill Michael could see what looked like another cluster of old military buildings.

Andrew started down the side trail leading down, saying, "This is the best part."

Michael held back. "I don't want to look at any more empty buildings," he said, sounding whinier than he liked. But he was feeling hot and dusty and tired.

"You'll really be missing something," his uncle said mildly. "This is the North Garrison. There's a museum inside. This used to be an immigration station. It was built nearly a century ago. People who came to California had to stop here before going on to the mainland. Some were let in; some were sent back where they came from; a few never left." A sad look crossed his face. "They died here, never reaching their new home, thousands of miles from where they were born."

"Kind of like Ellis Island in New York," said Michael. "We studied that in school."

"Yes. But most of the immigrants passing through Ellis Island were from Europe. Most of the people who stopped here were from Asia—mainly China. Great-Great Grandfather Choy came through here. Later his wife, your great-great grandmother, followed him to this place, then continued on to San Francisco. But did you know you had a great-uncle who died here years ago?"

"No," said Michael.

"Your great-great grandparents had been married in Canton. They had a child, a son named Li-wei, who was just about your age. When your great-great grandfather had saved up enough money, he brought his wife and child to America. They survived the trip across the Pacific in one of those crowded ships—there are pictures in the museum—but Li-wei didn't live long enough to cross the bay to San Francisco. Such a sad thing to think about."

"How did he die?" Michael wondered.

"Some wasting disease. Maybe he was already sick when they left Canton. Or he might have caught something during the ocean crossing. And the living quarters here were so crowded, germs could easily pass from one person to another. The story, supposedly told by his mother, was that he had a fever, and his throat got so swollen he couldn't eat anything. He could barely get a sip of water down. The infirmary couldn't do much more than apply cold compresses to break the fever, but nothing helped. He literally starved to death. Your great-great grandmother blamed herself. She thought her son had been possessed by a hungry ghost because, in her haste to prepare for the journey to California, she had not given the ancestors proper reverence. Though they had other children here, she never stopped grieving for Li-wei. But your great-uncle left his mark on this place. Curious, now?"

"Yes," Michael assured him. As they walked down the path, Michael found himself daydreaming. On the far side of the island, he had imagined soldiers' lonely lives turning to ghostly moonlight marching. Now he envisioned what it would have been like to be a boy—the same age as he—sick and dying after long days at sea, within sight of the city where his father waited for him: the home he would never reach. Surprised, Michael felt wetness in his eyes—tears for that boy who had died a century before. He couldn't imagine the pain and despair the boy must have felt, burning with fever, unable to eat, sucking on a wet washcloth when even a swallow of water choked him.

Michael suddenly touched his neck and swallowed anxiously, as if he feared his own throat might have closed up. And how did he know about the wet washcloth? he wondered. His uncle hadn't said anything. He pressed his hands to his cheeks. His face was burning, as if with fever. He was feeling lightheaded. Was he getting sick?

"It's cooler inside," said Andrew. "You look like you've had a little too much sun."

Michael shrugged. His imagination was working overtime, he assured himself, that was all.

The museum, it turned out, was in what had been the dormitory where men and women slept in separate quarters. How horrible it must have been for Li-wei, thought Michael. His long-dead great-uncle would have been separated from his mother at the time when he needed her most.

"There wasn't enough drinking water," said his uncle, his eyes skimming photo captions and displays as he refreshed his memory. "There were too few bathrooms. The food was awful." Now he sounded angry. Michael began to feel his own resentment grow as he moved around, taking things in. One photograph showed rows of Chinese women and infants seated on wall benches, facing each other across a narrow room. They were guarded by a prim white woman in a black uniform and hat. Another picture showed men and boys crowded into a dormitory, most sitting or stretched out on narrow metal bunks—three tiers high—with the thinnest of mattresses. The face of one boy, looking down from a top bed, seemed to gaze out of the picture, across time, into Michael's own eyes. He wondered if the boy had a fever. The eyes burned into his own with a hunger that made him look away. He moved to one side, then looked again, but still the eyes seemed to find his own, like those eerie portraits sold in Chinatown souvenir shops whose eyes followed you everywhere. Though the chance was remote, Michael fancied it was Li-wei who looked at him so. Probably he was already burning with fever, thirsty, hungry, *dying*—

A burst of pain, like a headache, but worse, made Michael press his hands to his temples. He turned and stepped back so suddenly he bumped into his uncle.

"Easy," Andrew said with a laugh. Then he looked more closely into his nephew's face. "You okay? Think you may have gotten a touch of sunstroke?" he asked worriedly.

"No. It's just—seeing all this. It's kind of bumming me out," said Michael, waving his hand to include the whole museum. "Why did the government allow people to be treated so badly?"

"You've heard enough history to know that back then lots of people didn't like the Chinese—for all we helped

build the railroads and make the West great. But back in those days, a lot of people were out of work, and the Chinese were blamed for taking jobs away. It wasn't true. There were lots of complicated reasons for the unemployment, but people never want hard truths, just easy answers. 'Too many Chinese,' was the easy reason for the hard times. 'The Chinese must go,' was the solution to the problem."

"Didn't anybody try to change things?"

"Who? The Chinese leaders had no real power. People were going broke and demanding that something be done. To keep a lid on things, the government made it harder for more Chinese to come into the country. So this place—supposedly the gateway to California—really was a closed door for most immigrants. Everyone who came here had to answer all sorts of questions to prove they were entering legally. Sometimes the questioning ran for months, even years. It was worse for your great uncle and great-great grandmother. There was a mix-up in papers or something: that's why they were kept here for months. That's probably why Li-wei died here."

The room was feeling hot and stuffy, yet Michael felt a chill. He was sure the eyes of the boy in the photograph were watching him hungrily. He suddenly wanted to be far away from this place, the awful displays, the feverish eyes.

"One more thing to show you," his uncle said. Carved on the walls of the men's dormitory were the up-and-down lines of Chinese characters. Michael knew enough to recognize these as poems. Some expressed sadness at having left home in search of the "Land of the Golden Mountains"—the boy knew this meant "California"—while most expressed anger at being kept in misery, fenced in by barbed wire, being endlessly questioned, never knowing their fate.

"This is the one I want you to see," said his uncle.

In a corner, carved at a height that made it easy for him to read, was a poem. Michael read,

My father waits for me in
The Land of Golden Mountains;
My mother has been taken from me.
I have done nothing wrong;
Still I am held in this wooden house
For several tens of days
Fatherless, motherless—
A criminal who has done no crime.
My skin burns; my eyes fill with tears;
I am thirsty and hungry all the time.
I will never reach
The Land of Golden Mountains.
I beg whoever reads this
To remember Choy Li-wei.

Michael read it over again, his uncle helping him with difficult words. Suddenly the carved characters seemed to blaze red-gold, almost blinding him, though neither his uncle nor the one or two other visitors noticed. The boy closed his eyes but found the words burning in the darkness behind his lids. His ancestor's poem, his hunger to be remembered, had burned itself into Michael's consciousness. He would never forget the poem, he knew. He would never forget—anything.

The stuffy air in the place made him dizzy. He swayed a bit. Uncle Andrew threw an arm around his shoulder to steady him.

"Can we go?" Michael asked, wiping his eyes that felt scorched by the lines of the poem that now was once again just antique carving on a rough wooden wall.

Outside, his uncle said, "Do you want to sit down?"

"No. I just want to go. I'll just have some water. And something to eat." He finished off the last of his own bottle, then his uncle's water. Eagerly he wolfed down the half-packet of Tic-Tacs his uncle found in a pocket. He felt desperately hungry and thirsty—as if he hadn't stuffed himself at the picnic just a short time before.

As they returned to the main trail, Andrew glanced at his watch. "Uh-oh! We're cutting it pretty close. We'll have to take the shorter, steeper trail down to the ferry landing." Michael, his skin burning, followed his uncle without answering.

Even taking the shortcut, they barely reached the dock before the last ferry pulled out. Their family, gathered on the dock, surrounded by picnic supplies and folding chairs, waved and shouted and scolded the two stragglers. Uncle Andrew apologized, taking the blame on himself.

As the boat pulled away from the pier, Michael sat by himself in the darkest corner of the inside cabin. But even here he felt as hot as if he were standing in the full glare of the sun. His stomach growled with hunger; his throat felt dust-dry. He spent the last of his pocket money on bottled water and cookies at the snack bar. "You'll get fat," teased his Aunt Violet as she passed him. But he only looked down at the empty cookie packet thinking that he was so hungry he would never feel filled up, let alone fat.

Suddenly he stood up and walked out to the front of the ferry, holding on to the railing because he felt so unsteady. He was glad his relatives were so busy talking and enjoying the return trip that they didn't notice his distress. Outside he leaned over the railing, watching Angel Island disappear behind them. He would never go back, he knew. As the distance grew between that place and him, Michael felt like a man freed from prison. The depth of his feelings surprised him. The single visit to the museum—surely they hadn't been there more than half an hour?—had stirred up his emotions to a degree that made no sense to him, as he felt waves of anger, joy, pain, and hope flooding him. It was like tapping into someone else's feelings.

Two of his younger cousins, sitting on one of the open-air benches at the front of the ferry, called to him. He ignored them. The only thing in his mind was going as far forward as the railings would allow. When he could go no further without climbing the guardrail, he grabbed it with both hands, and leaned eagerly into the wind. It stung his face, making his forehead and cheeks and hands burn even more. But he didn't care.

The wind purified him. He felt a part of himself swept away by the wind, like so many old rags. The clutter of

Michael's memories, hopes, ambitions scattered like dry leaves, leaving his soul empty and hungry. But the boy soon found a feast of other thoughts and dreams and memories to fill the emptiness.

San Francisco lay directly ahead. The sinking sun beyond the Golden Gate was tinting the tips of the city's towers and hills gold. And he was going home at last. After so many thousands of days, he was nearing his journey's end. He thought some children were calling to him, but he didn't recognize the name they used, so he paid no attention. The fever on his skin was cooling; his thirst was fading; even the ghostly hunger that had tormented him was going. For the first time in ages, he felt filled. He possessed a body again, exploring it the way someone would explore a house after the earlier owners had moved out. And the former owner of this house? Gone: his soul swallowed by a hunger that stretched across time. Some little part of what had been there remained—a memory here, a bit of dream there. But these would help him settle into his new life as he finally reached journey's end, came home.

This time, when the children called "Michael," Li-wei turned and smiled and waved back.

Bak Otahl

As far as Marty was concerned, the town of Hualapai was the dullest place in Arizona, in the U.S.A., in the *world*. There were still times he couldn't believe his father, Everett Branders, the up-and-coming sculptor, had moved the two of them from Connecticut to downtown no-where here in the desert. If it hadn't been for his friends Connor, Wayne, and Mojo (Michael Joseph to his parents), his dirt bike, and some of the girls at Fess Parker Middle School, he'd have run screaming into the desert long ago.

"Inspiration," said his father, when the boy challenged the move to the adobe house on the edge of the sun-baked town. "I'm going to find ideas for great new sculptures here. The desert has always inspired artists."

"It inspires boredom," said Marty, making a big show of stifling a yawn.

"You're too smart for your own good," said his father good-naturedly. "No twelve-year-old should have as many answers as you do. You're gifted."

"It's no great gift to recognize *boooorrrrrring*," Marty said.

"Live with it," said his father. "I have this place for a year."

Marty knew that was only part of it. The change in their living situation had moved them out of the house where Marty's mother had died. Every room, every corner of the garden, was filled with memories of her. His father had been frozen in sorrow for a long time; the move to Hualapai had been a way to get his stalled career moving again. Marty was sharp enough to realize this, so he didn't harp too much on how dull he found the town.

Every day, his father would go happily off to the shed that had become his studio to work with metal and acetylene, turning his inspirations into the massive sculptures he was becoming well known for. Right now, he was working on a giant piece called "Bakotahl Arising." It was inspired by stories of a devil the Indians said lived under a nearby mountain range and sometimes broke free to bring evil into the world.

Marty put his energy into finding ways to keep boredom at bay. This Saturday, he sat on the front steps, black helmet with gold stars in his lap, dirt bike—the Kawasaki KLX110, a bribe from his father to keep him from complaining too loudly—leaning against the porch. He was waiting for his friends to show up. Pretty soon he saw them—first as dust plumes whipping along like three dust-devils scudding single-file across the sandy desert floor dotted with the various green shades of mesquite, sage, yucca, and an occasional tall, twisted Joshua tree.

Then he heard the *buzzroar* of their desert bikes. Finally he saw the three helmeted boys, each crouched low over his bike's handlebars, following one of the rutted paths, away from the real roads, they had cut in the past weeks, traveling between Marty's house and the town a quarter-mile away. Wayne was in the lead, naturally; Connor was right behind him; Mojo, as usual, brought up the rear, trailing the others by a good hundred yards. Their bright-colored helmets, jackets, boots, and gloves gave them the look of freshly landed starship troopers.

The first two boys brought their bikes to a smooth halt with a minimum of dust flurries.

"Yo, bro!" cried Wayne, flipping up the clear visor on his skull-and-crossbones-decorated helmet.

Connor waved and pulled his candy-apple-green-with-a-white-stripe helmet off. Fishing a rag from his back pocket, he began to rub squashed insects off his visor. Then Mojo arrived, tried to execute a wheelie, nearly lost control of his bike showing off, and raised a cloud of dust that billowed over the other boys.

"Mojo, you doofus!" Wayne shouted.

"Sorry, guys." Mojo shrugged and grinned.

"Hey, Mojo," said Marty, "do you know you got a big gob of bird crap on your helmet?"

"Oh, yeah! I meant to clean it off earlier. Can I borrow your rag, Connor?"

"I guess." Connor, his visor polished up, handed over the cleaning cloth. Mojo removed his helmet and set to work cleaning the white-green spatter from between the horns of the grinning devil logo on his Arizona State Sun Devils helmet. When he was done, he tried to return the rag to Connor. But the other boy just wrinkled his nose and said, "I don't want that crapped-up thing. You keep it." Mojo shrugged and shoved it into his jacket pocket. The other three boys just grinned at each other and shook their heads.

"Everybody ready?" asked Wayne.

Marty climbed onto his Kawasaki, put on his helmet, and gave a thumbs-up sign. The other four bikes—Yamahas and a Honda—roared to life, then sped down the dirt road to the cutoff from the highway fifty yards past the house Marty's father had rented. It cut arrow-straight through the scrub to a farm owned by an Indian family, the Nunezes, who raised traditional foods: corn, melons, mesquite beans, and pumpkins. The Nunez boys, twins, were in Marty's homeroom at school. They kept to themselves and were often the butt of jokes and rough-housing by the other boys. Marty had joined in the hazing from time to time. He found he liked being a bully—especially when he had a circle of friends to back him up. The Indians' standoffishness, their unwillingness to fight back, their refusal to plead or to cry, the way they would simply stare at their tormentors with their dark eyes—these traits brought out the worst in their classmates. No amount of lecturing from teachers or counselors changed anything. Duane and Dano—their anglo names: no one knew their Indian names—were the class punching bags, and nothing would change that.

As the four boys raced down the road, Marty now third and Mojo eating his dust, Marty almost hoped they'd run into the twins. A little scuffling would liven up the morning. But he knew they were probably hard at work on the farm. Sometimes, when they were heading to their favorite riding area at the foot of the low mountain range dead ahead, Marty and the others would recognize the Nunez boys working in the fields.

Today, as they dusted past the fence that marked the edge of the farm, they saw no one. Marty guessed that work was going on in the fields that extended farther south toward the reservation, from which extra field hands were hired as needed. The family never hired anyone but Indians, though there were plenty of guys in Hualapai who could use the work, Marty knew. This added to the town's general dislike of the Nunezes—something Marty had been quick to pick up on even during his short time in the area.

Ahead were the rugged white granite bluffs named the Devil's Gathering, so called because at certain times of the day the pale peaks and slopes revealed the shapes of ghosts, skulls, ogres, and, on the highest peak, a one-horned devil lording it over the rest. In geography class, Mr. Mathers had explained that the local Indians still called it by the name Bakotahl, after the evil spirit who supposedly slept underneath. Realizing this was the same story that had inspired his father's latest sculpture, Marty had listened with real interest. He learned that

Bakotahl's twin, the good Creator, had forced the devilish Bakotahl underground. In the past, when he awoke, he had caused earthquakes so bad that the mountain walls cracked and the earth split open. He could call down thunder and raise deadly whirlwinds. There was no end to the evil he might do. To the local tribes, Bakotahl remained a sacred place, a sign of the power of good and a warning that evil may sleep for a time without ever really leaving the earth.

To Marty and his pals, however, the lowest slopes of the bluffs were an excellent arena for testing the power of their bikes and their own skill and nerve. They had crisscrossed the area with bike trails. It was their special place. They discouraged others from using it. Only a week before, they'd run off a pack of elementary-school kids who had trespassed with their little *putt-putt* scooters.

They roared into their space, crisscrossing behind and in front of each other, then riding parallel. Sometimes they came dangerously close to colliding—especially when Mojo was involved—but this only added spice to their maneuvers. Marty, Wayne, and Connor pushed themselves and their bikes to the extreme. Mojo kept to the easier trails, the safer leaps. "Mojo, the no-go!" Marty yelled when the smaller boy veered away from what should have been a fairly easy fly-over of a narrow but deep fissure. Wayne and Connor took up the chant, "No-go, Mojo!" Marty and the others were amused to see their friend torn between his fear of the leap and his fear that his friends would brand him "No-go" forever. Caught between these wretched alternatives, Mojo began to glance everywhere, as if to find a way out of the trap. Above them, the sun, nearing its noon high, changed the shadow patterns on the bluffs, so it seemed that a ghost and a troll and the one-horned devil were all smirking at Mojo.

"Hey! Who's that?" Mojo shouted—pointing to a boulder that had tumbled free of the cliffs in some past age. The other three turned in time to see a dark-haired boy duck down behind the rock from where he had been watching the friends' motocross.

Wayne gunned his engine, starting up the trail to the left of the boulder, signaling to Marty, who was just behind him, to take the right-hand trail. Marty saw at once that this was a flanking action to cut off the spy's escape. Connor followed Wayne; Mojo tailed Marty. All four were yelling, excited by the hunt. In his eagerness to catch the spy, Marty nearly ran head-on into Wayne, as the two rounded the boulder, braked, and spun away from each other in the flat stretch behind the massive rock.

"There he goes!" shouted Marty. Their quarry was taking the only way of escape: running up the trail that sliced between towering granite walls.

"It's one of the Nunez freaks," Marty shouted over the sound of all four engines idling furiously.

"Which one?" asked Wayne.

"How should I know? They look the same. Who cares? Let's give whichever one it is such a scare that the other will wet his pants." Marty revved his bike a few more times, pleased that the sound made the runner pause and look back at his pursuers. He imagined he saw fear in the boy's face; then the boy turned away and ran even faster.

"He's mine!" yelled Marty, taking the lead before Wayne could protest. His bike blasted up the trail, scattering gravel that rebounded off the trail walls and peppered Wayne, who protested in a bellow, but didn't slow down. Behind him, Connor and Mojo lifted their faces to the cloud-flecked sky and howled like wolves scenting blood.

The trail twisted and turned, so Marty and the others had to slow to avoid slamming into the rock walls. And they had to slow again as the trail narrowed. But Marty wasn't worried: he knew the other boy was trapped. Not much farther along, the trail suddenly widened into a natural bowl, which was split from side to side by a deep crack that looked like it dropped into the granite heart of the Devil's Gathering. Remembering Mr. Mathers's class and his father's work, Marty had christened it Bakotahl's Challenge. At some point, one of them, revving up courage (and maybe a more powerful bike) would dare the fly-over. But not yet. The distance and depth were too daunting—even for Marty, the most daredevil of the four. So escape that way was cut off for someone on foot. And the floor of the bowl sloped gently upward at first—then shot up so steeply and smoothly that climbing was impossible. The Indian spy was trapped. They'd give him the scare of his life, Marty thought, before they left him—with maybe a black eye and a bloody nose for souvenirs.

The other boy, his white shirt flapping over his dusty jeans, kept running toward the other side. Marty knew that in a minute he'd stop, aware of the drop-off, discovering there was no escape.

Marty had brought his bike to a halt just beyond the entrance to the bowl, but he kept the motor idling feverishly. Wayne pulled up beside him a few seconds later. Then Connor and Mojo. They formed a ragged line.

"Go!" ordered Marty, who now realized that he, not Wayne, was going to be the leader of their pack from now on. "Scare the crap out of the creep!"

He set the pace. The four rolled down the slope toward the floor of the open area. Marty howled. They all howled.

Ahead, the boy ran without slowing.

Then he disappeared. Marty saw him extend his arms, his wind-whipped sleeves like wings. For a crazy instant, he thought the Indian boy might fly all the way over Bakotahl's Challenge. But his seeming flight became a deadly arc downward. The boy gave a scream, as if he suddenly realized what was happening.

Marty barely wheeled his bike around short of the drop-off. Wayne narrowly avoided the same danger by swerving so sharply his bike skidded sideways, leaving Wayne in the dirt while the bike came to rest in a clump of yucca, its engine still racing. Connor managed to hit his brakes; then Mojo crashed into Connor, leaving the boys and their bikes in a tangle.

For a moment, there was just the sound of groaning riders and racing engines, as dust whirled around them. Then, one by one, they killed their engines. For a few minutes, no one spoke as the dust settled around them.

His friends looked lost, so Marty took control of the situation.

"He fell," said Marty. His voice sounded steady though his legs felt wobbly.

"We killed him," said Wayne. "We ran him right off the edge." He started to cry.

"Mojo ran into me," said Connor, as if this was all he was aware of.

"Shut up!" Marty warned them all. "We'd better see what happened."

He walked to the edge of the ravine, the others following several paces behind. Far below, the boy lay partly on a ledge, his head and left arm dangling into space.

"We've got to get help," whispered Wayne.

"He's not moving," said Marty. "No one can help him."

Still they stood for nearly five minutes watching. But not a finger or an eyelid twitched.

"Will we go to jail?" asked Mojo, who had also started to cry.

"Don't be stupid," Marty insisted. "We didn't do anything. He didn't look where he was going, and he fell. No one will blame us."

"Sure they will," said Connor. "When they find out, we're all gonna wind up in detention hall. Maybe jail, since he's dead."

"There's no need for anyone to find out, if you keep your mouths shut." Marty's mind was working overtime now. "There's nothing to connect us to his accident."

"Our tire tracks are all over the place," said Wayne, brushing aside his tears.

"We come up here all the time. Everyone knows that. And we never touched him—never even got near him. There's nothing to tie us to him, unless one of you opens your mouth. And I promise you, if you do, you'll be dead meat before the sheriff can get to you. Now let's get out of here. We'll go and mess around by Apache Creek for a while, then go home. If anyone asks where we were today, just tell them we were at the creek."

They followed the plan. It was painless for Marty. His father was so wrapped up in "Bakotahl Arising" that he stayed out in his studio long after Marty had fixed dinner for both of them. Exhausted, he hardly spoke two words to his son before falling asleep on the couch.

Marty, glad to have the time to himself, went upstairs. He tried a couple of computer games, then surfed the television in his room just to be doing something. But he couldn't get rid of the image of the boy seeming to take flight, then dropping with a single terrified cry.

He stayed awake most of the night. Toward dawn, there were loud rumblings of thunder over the Devil's Gathering. But the morning itself was sunny, with no hint of a storm.

Sunday he stayed around the house. His father was surprised that he wasn't out with his friends on their bikes, but he welcomed the company when Marty just sat and watched him sculpting the huge image of the demonic figure climbing out of a mountain like a monster hatching from an egg. Marty found the subject creepy, but the silence of the house and his memories of the day before were far more disturbing. Distant, rainless thunder again kept him awake most of the night.

On Monday, the school was abuzz with rumors that Dano Nunez had run away or been kidnapped. While Marty was getting his books out of his locker, he was suddenly aware that Duane Nunez was staring at him from across the hall. It was as if the other boy were trying to size him up or see inside his head. He started to challenge the Indian boy, then thought better of it and turned away. But all through the day he was aware of the Indian boy watching him. Sometimes he caught him staring at Wayne or Connor or Mojo. By a kind of silent agreement, the four friends didn't speak to each other. Even when Marty got his customary ride home from Connor's brother, he and Connor sat silently in the back seat, each staring out a window at opposite sides of the road.

On the following Friday, a search party found Dano Nunez's body. No one knew who heard it first, but everyone in the school knew by lunchtime. The following week the local newspaper reported that "the cause of the boy's death is being investigated." But nothing came of it. It was nothing more disturbing than the nightly thunderstorms over the Devil's Gathering.

Duane Nunez was gone for several days—presumably for the funeral. Marty was glad to have him away, since he was always aware of the boy watching him and the others. And he didn't dare say anything, for fear of where a confrontation might lead. Things might be said in the heat of an argument that they'd all regret.

Gradually, life returned to normal. The boys took up their dirt biking again—though they stayed away from the Devil's Gathering. At home, Everett Branders's sculpture grew into a towering nightmare—Bakotahl bursting triumphantly from his prison deep in a mountain—as Marty's father poured all of his passion and energy into his creation.

Duane Nunez returned for a single day to school. While Marty was sitting in homeroom, the Indian boy passed him and leaned over and whispered in his ear the single word, "Bakotahl."

After school, Marty found out that the same thing had happened to Wayne, Connor, and Mojo. They decided they would find Duane and force him to tell what he meant by the word. But they couldn't find him. He was gone the next day, his locker cleaned out; their homeroom teacher explained simply that Duane's parents were going to homeschool him.

What he had been trying to say or threaten would remain a mystery to the four friends.

Not long after this, they took their bikes north to a series of bluffs that were separate from the Devil's Gathering. But there were some challenging trails there, weaving in and out of the boulder-strewn slopes. It was a good day, with plenty of chance for everyone but Mojo—who stayed on what the others called "the bunny slopes"—to do some truly extreme riding. They roared and raced through the early afternoon. As the sun was beginning to set, and they were thinking of heading home, Wayne decided to tackle one more impressive fly-over of a deep gash in the earth. Thunder was rumbling over these mountains the way it did so often over the Devil's Gathering these days. It grew louder and louder as Wayne prepared for his jump. Marty began to wonder if there would truly be rain this time; that always posed the danger of flash floods. "Let's head out," he said to Wayne.

"One last time," Wayne said. He revved his engine, then shot toward the crack. At the same moment, the thunder shook the rocks around them so fiercely it knocked Marty's parked bike on its side. Connor and Mojo had better luck steadying their own bikes.

"Earthquake!" Marty shouted. The earth heaved. Then, just as Wayne raced up the packed-dirt ramp and launched himself into the air, the earth roared and ripped the narrow chasm five times as wide as it had been. There was no time to shout a warning; there was nothing the others could do but watch as Wayne and his bike fell far short of the still-shaking ground on the other side and plummeted. Wayne held on to his handlebars as if he could somehow guide himself to safety. Marty remembered Dano Nunez's arms straining to become wings to carry him. It was a nightmare replayed. The earth stopped shaking, but the thunder persisted, dying away with a sound that reminded Marty eerily of fading laughter.

Wayne's body and bike weren't recovered until late that night. The boys were not at the site when emergency rescue teams brought them up. Each was home, being consoled by their families, who didn't know that they were not just reacting to Wayne's death, but reliving the secret tragedy of two months earlier.

After a few days, Marty and Connor returned to school. Mojo didn't turn up until two days later. When they saw him, they were shocked at how bad he looked. His face was pale and his eyes were ringed with dark circles, as if he hadn't slept. At first he tried to avoid the other boys, but they cornered him on the playground.

"What's up?" asked Marty. "You won't talk to us, and you look worse than roadkill."

"I'm afraid."

"Of what?" Connor asked.

"Bakotahl killed Wayne," Mojo said. "I think he's going to get us all. For what we did to Dano. Maybe Duane called him up with some Indian magic."

Marty began to laugh. "You've been watching too many movies. Indian spirits. Evil from the burial ground. We've all watched *The Manitou* and crap like that on *Creature Features*."

"I think it's true," said Mojo. He wasn't arguing; he just sounded hopeless.

"Bull!" said Connor. But his eyes suggested he wasn't as sure as he sounded.

"Double bull!" said Marty. "You're sick and imagining things." Then he grabbed Mojo's arm and squeezed hard.

"Have you told them anything about—you know?" *Harder.* "Have you?"

"I swear I haven't. I just tell them I'm having nightmares. They wouldn't believe me anyway. Don't worry," he added bitterly. "It won't be *me* who gets you guys in trouble."

"Meaning?"

"I've got to go. Tomorrow my folks are taking me to Kingman to see some special doctors."

"All you need is the right pill," said Marty. "And a good night's sleep."

But Mojo was already walking away and didn't hear.

The wall phone in the kitchen rang two nights later, while Marty and his father were cleaning up the dinner dishes. Everett grabbed the phone off the wall, listened for a moment, then handed the receiver to his son. "Connor," he said. "I'm going to watch TV." He left.

"What's up?" asked Marty.

"Mojo's dead!" said Connor. "My mother heard it on the news today. There was a bad accident on the road to Kingman yesterday. Some kind of huge dust storm blew across the road and dumped tons of sand on things. Cars and trucks went everywhere. An RV skidded and hit the car Mojo was riding in with his mom and dad. His folks may make it, but Mojo didn't."

Marty said nothing for a minute. Connor was equally quiet. It was Connor who broke the silence.

"I think Mojo was right. Remember how Duane whispered 'Bakotahl' to each of us. I think he was warning us; or maybe that was how he put a curse on us. But I've been thinking about that story Mr. Mathers told us. How Bakotahl can make earthquakes and whirlwinds. Well, those are what got Wayne and now Mojo. One of us will be next."

"That's garbage," said Marty.

"I'm going to tell what we did to Dano," said Connor. "Maybe telling will put an end to this."

"Don't do anything yet. I've got to think." Marty heard the TV click on in the next room.

"I've got to go," he said. "But we need to talk. You come over here: there are too many of your family around all the time at your place."

"How?" asked Connor. "It's nighttime, and I've been grounded for a couple of days. My brother can't drive me: he's at a party somewhere."

"Use your bike," said Marty. "It's a full moon. We've done plenty of riding at night. Just be sure to walk your bike in so my dad doesn't hear. Meet me out in my father's studio."

"Talking won't do any good," said Connor.

"Just be here." Marty hung up the phone.

He needn't have worried about his father. True to form, Everett had fallen asleep ten minutes into a PBS documentary. Marty sat and watched awhile to kill time. Sure that his father would sleep on, he left the house.

There was the familiar sound of thunder—but this time it seemed to come from overhead—not just from the sky over the Devil's Gathering. And the air was heavy with the promise of rain. Earlier that day, Marty had seen blue-black rain veils to the south—over the reservation. Just before dark the rain clouds, laced with violet lightning, had drifted closer—as close as the Nunez farm.

Thinking of the farm made him think of Duane. *Freak!* Thought Marty. Putting the seed of fear in their ears with his whispered "Bakotahl." Somewhere Marty had read how witch doctors made a person grow sick and die just by telling them this would happen. After that, a person's own fear made the threat come true. He'd just have to make Connor see that he was playing into the Indian's hands by letting fear run away with him. What happened to Wayne was freaky. But earthquakes happened—look at California! And Mojo was half-dead with fright. His parents were scared for him. That might have made whoever was driving the car much less able to deal with the dust storm. But sandstorms and dust devils were a fact of desert life. Not an Indian curse.

Clouds were massing overhead, blotting out the moon and stars. Lightning crackled. Marty hoped the rain would hold off until Connor arrived. It would probably blow over quickly, as most desert storms did. His fear was that Connor would turn back to avoid the rain.

He let himself in to the studio. The statue of Bakotahl was nearly completed. Even to Marty, who had seen a lot of his father's sculptures, the size was incredible. The shed had a high roof—nearly two stories—with a skylight that made it an ideal studio space. The upstretched metal claws of the emerging demon almost touched the overhead glass. It's going to take a moving van to get this sucker to a gallery or museum, Marty thought. He sat himself on the lowest slope of the sculpted mountain, facing the door.

Rain began drumming on the roof and skylight. Soon the skylight well was covered with water so that, looking up, Marty had the impression of being undersea. Now the demon seemed to be swimming toward the surface of some dark ocean. The rain fell more heavily. The thunder and lightning jolted him.

Marty was about to give up on Connor, when the shed door opened, and Connor walked his bike in, leaving a trail of mud and wet sand behind.

"Don't bring that in here! It's my Dad's *studio!*"

Connor ignored him, putting down the kickstand, then pulling off his helmet and gloves and shaking the rain off them. He carefully hung them from the handlebars. Only when he had done this, did he look directly at Marty and say, "All right. Talk."

Marty, still lounging at the base of the statue, launched into his argument about how fear and freak accidents were making Connor the victim of Duane's so-called curse.

"He knew what happened to his brother," said Connor.

"How? There was no one around but Dano and us. He was *guessing*."

"He was a twin. Twins know when things happen to each other. Someone told me that a long time ago."

"If he knew, why didn't he tell the sheriff?"

"Indians are different. They do things their own way. I think we've got to tell the truth. Maybe we can stop—"

He didn't finish his sentence, as if saying aloud what he was afraid of might make it happen.

"Stop what?" Marty sneered. "This guy?" He rapped with his knuckles on the statue behind him. It made a hollow, booming sound that was echoed by a fresh roll of thunder outside. Rain hissed and boiled on the roof and skylight; wind-driven, it battered the windows and poured down in rippling sheets sometimes backlit by lightning. The wind rattled the windows and door as if trying to get in.

"That's a monster storm out there," said Marty, trying to break the tension.

"I'm telling," said Connor stubbornly.

"No!" Marty lunged at him, grabbing him by the corner of his jacket.

"Let go!" Connor shoved Marty away.

"Don't push me, you—" Marty was really angry now. He caught Connor's waist in a tackle that sent them both slamming into Connor's bike, tipping it over. The two boys, rolling around the floor, punching at each other, hardly noticed.

The rain fell now with a sound like a waterfall—as if the heavens were emptying a sky full of rain onto the shed roof.

Still the boys battered each other. They didn't stop even when their tussling took them near the shed door and they rolled through a widening puddle, as storm-driven water, mixed with dirt and sand, gushed through the gap under the door.

Panting, Marty broke free and staggered to his feet. Connor also tried to gain his footing, but he slipped in the puddling water on the cement floor. Marty took advantage of the other boy's unsteadiness and slammed him with his shoulder. Connor's feet slid out from under him, and he fell back onto the base of the statue, hitting his head. He sprawled there, like some offering at a monstrous altar.

Marty, his anger turning to fear, looked down at his unconscious friend. He knelt beside the other boy. "Connor?" he called.

For a moment he felt himself trapped in a nightmare: Connor dead. Himself the killer. The demon grinning overhead. Rain pouring down and flooding in like it would never end.

Then Connor groaned and rubbed the back of his head. He opened his eyes. Marty began to let the fear seep out of him. "Sorry," he said. He put his hand out to help Connor up. This wasn't some awful part of an Indian curse; it was just a couple of hot tempers flaring. Maybe now Connor would listen, Marty thought. He can't go anywhere in the storm.

Impossibly, the storm intensified. There was a sudden surge of water that reached almost to the base of the windows.

"Flash flood!" Marty yelled, as water jetted in through cracks and holes in the weathered siding of the shed.

"Bakotahl," said Connor, in the hopeless tone of voice Marty had earlier heard Mojo use.

For a minute, he imagined the shed being swept away, with them swirled in the wreckage like so much debris. He could almost see their drowned selves being discovered days from now in some flood-formed gully, half buried in caked desert sand.

Then the rain eased up. The flooding water subsided.

"So much for the curse," said Marty, beginning to laugh with relief. Connor joined in the frantic laughter, too. The studio was filled with their laughter, when the floor, undermined by the flood, suddenly buckled. The massive sculpture of Bakotahl pitched forward and down, crushing the boys as they scrambled to escape.